BEDTIME STORIES

for big boys & girls

with special bonus material from…
EROTIC DREAMS AND SATIN SHEETS
and
Secret Liaisons
and
SEDUCTION: An Erotic Multimedia Experience

by

Gabrielle Elise

Dedication

This book contains a collection of short stories and fantasies for both men and women to either enjoy separately or together. I hope that you enjoy reading them as much as I did writing them.

-Gabrielle Elise

Acknowledgements

I would like to thank the following people who have encouraged and supported me over the years, and who have inspired the imagination that helped me to create my stories.

Pat – thank you for encouraging me in the first place to continue writing and for being such a good friend. I'd like to thank Kerry, Roxane, Anne, Joy, Donna, Pammy, Cindy, Sami, Dawn and my Sisters Michaela and Laura for being such awesome girlfriends and for accepting me for who I am and still liking me anyway!

Special thanks to all the people who have touched my life over the years; it's all of you who make my life such an incredible place to be! Bob, thank you for being the one man in my life who has always believed in me and made me feel good about myself and most of all, thank you for allowing me to write on "your time!" Cathy – you've been a mom to me for so many years. I love you and thank you. Naomi – my guardian angel. Thank you for everything. Mathew and Julissa – I love you more than anything else in the world. I love you all and I am so lucky to have you in my life.

First Print Edition (2002)

One Night Stand

As I stood in the bar watching the band, he came up behind me and whispered in my ear, "I want to lick you like no one has ever licked you before."

When I turned around, I recognized him as the cute young thing I talked to earlier.

The night lingered on and the drinks continued. And still the little guy didn't give up. An hour later he approached me again, his eyes locked on mine. "This could be the best night of your life," he whispered. "When I'm finished with you, you're going to beg me for more."

Truth is, I wanted to find out. He'd piqued my curiosity.

The bar closed at 1:30 A.M. We all headed for the door, and, before I knew it, I was standing at my car, trying to say goodbye to this sexy young man. He was taller than me so I had to lift my head to see his face. Over his beautiful blue eyes were lashes that seemed to last forever. His full lips beckoned kisses and formed a persuasive smile – a smile that might talk me into anything. Of course I agreed to go home with him.

He lived in a tiny one-room apartment, sparsely furnished: a queen-sized bed that dominated the center of the room and a table by the door with an antique candleholder. I saw they were burnt down to nubs, but he ceremoniously lit them anyway. Soon their soothing light danced playfully across the bare walls.

I watched him go to the refrigerator to get us both a beer. From his broad shoulders, his long torso tapered down his back to a small waist and an ass I desperately wanted to grab. He seemed to appreciate my attentions as he returned and handed me my beer. A moment later he put his beer down on the table and took his shirt off. My body started to tremble as I looked at his tanned chest. He was beautiful.

Slowly, he walked around the table to me, took the beer from my hand and placed it next to his. He looked into my eyes, and said, "I'm going to show you what I was talking about. I'm going to lick you until you scream out my name and beg me to enter you. And then we'll make love all night long… until our bodies are too weak to move."

He began to disrobe me, pausing to smile with each article of clothing, as he considered my body in the candlelight. He touched me, his fingers complementing my soft skin as he kissed me on my shoulders and neck. My body ached for him. I was wet and throbbing, and he was driving me crazy. We drifted over to the bed.

As we lay down on the bed, he parted my legs and, as promised, started to lick me in a way I'd never experienced before – slowly at first, moving his tongue over the edges of my lips, then moving in deeper, as far as it could go.

His tongue made love to me, sending my body into orgasmic spasms until I felt a flood of juices flow out of me and into his mouth. When he finished licking me, he kissed my stomach, trailing his tongue up towards my breasts biting and sucking on each nipple. My body screamed for him and before I knew it, so was I.

I offered to reciprocate, but he wouldn't allow it. He wanted to spend the entire evening pleasing me.

He pulled me up towards him, placing me on his lap. I wrapped my legs around his waist and we kissed for the first time. He twisted my body until he could comfortably enter me. He felt so good inside me as he moved up and down, his pace increasing with every thrust. Faster and faster. Soon, he began moaning – quietly, then louder, then louder still. Then I felt his body jerking around uncontrollably. He suddenly pulled out of me, and squirted cum all over my stomach. We lay on the sweat-soaked sheets for an indeterminate time, our syncopated breathing pulsing throughout the room. Only one candle burned, the room a shade lighter than dark, but I could still see the splash of cum on my stomach and the hairs on his chest glistening from his sweat.

Hours later I awoke in dawn light to his suckling my breasts and rubbing his fingers between my legs. He was quite an energetic young thing. I reminded myself of our age difference, smiled, and wanted him again. I told him so.

He went back down between my legs and began licking, this time inserting his finger. The combined exertions of tongue and digit amazed, and stirred feelings in me that shook my world. I felt hot everywhere and beads of sweat rolled off my forehead.

I didn't know whether to laugh or cry. My emotions were out-of-whack; my body had left on the ride without me and was completely enjoying itself. The experience was incredible – unlike any I'd ever had. I came in explosive exhaustion, my body aching and paralyzed. The moment was at once exciting and frightening. It was everything I'd ever imagined. More.

He was right: he may have been young, but he was definitely gifted.

I ducked out while he was still asleep. After a brief heated inner debate, I chose not to leave my telephone number. Though tempted to, in the back of my mind, I knew this incredible experience could never be repeated.

The Possibilities Are Endless

When he walked into the coffee shop, she couldn't help but notice him – his muscular shoulders, solid tanned legs, and gorgeous smile. He had dark black hair, a thick black mustache and eyes the color of the Caribbean Ocean.

Taylor came in here every morning for a decaf mocha with non-fat milk. And for the past two weeks, this tall, dark, and handsome man had also come in, his drink of choice, a large double espresso and a scone. She would watch him, following his every move. While he ordered, he would smile at the cashier until he received his coffee, and then would quickly walk out the door. When he passed her table, she could smell the strong scent of Calvin Klein's *Eternity*. He wore it well, and it would linger in the air long after he'd left. He walked with elegance and grace, and was always dressed nicely in tailored slacks, a Polo shirt, and shiny leather loafers. It was obvious he had expensive tastes to go with his perfect sense of style.

One day, as Taylor sat in the shop reading, the handsome stranger departed routine. As he headed up to the counter, he smiled at her, and even said hello. Then, when he'd gotten his coffee, he came back to her table and asked if he could join her. She nodded.

He introduced himself as Wade, and for the next hour, they talked easily – about everything and nothing. Wade was funny and smart and, well, sexy, she thought. As she sat so close to him, she could feel her face flush and her skin moisten with perspiration. He made her a little nervous. And aroused. Wade was a very sexy man.

While he talked, she absorbed his presence, his words becoming mere sounds, senseless. She imagined herself and him together on a beach, holding hands, laughing, kissing, playing in the water. He talked, she imagined. Their clothes came off as they playfully wrestled together on the sand. Then they hungrily attacked one another. As they lay there on the sand, spent, the ocean waves lapped up around them, and swept over their naked bodies.

Drifting back into the conversation, her heart still racing from her thought dream, she registered some meaning from him. It seemed Wade owned a skydiving company. Excitedly, she remarked to him that she had wanted to try skydiving for quite some time. In fact, she added, it was her recent first-time episode with bungee jumping that had re-sparked this interest. The free fall was a rush, she said.

They talked a little longer, and as he was getting ready to leave, he asked her if she wanted to go with him on a jump the following day. Without hesitation, she said, "yes," and they made plans to meet at his office early the next morning.

They met the next day at the airfield where he gave her the necessary preliminary lessons before they boarded the plane. In the air, while she sat across from him, she drifted. She pictured herself with Wade, making love on a bed of parachutes, their naked bodies intertwined in the ropes and silky-soft, colored fabric – stuck together in humid wetness while they screamed out their mutual pleasure.

Before her thoughts reached the point of no return, she heard Wade asking her if she was ready. "Yes, yes I am ready, Wade."

But not for what you're talking about, she thought.

The dive was exhilarating – electric, exciting – an incredible experience. When she touched the ground, she shivered as the parachute slowly fell around her.

Wade, who had dived seconds after she, came running to her, offered his hand and asked if she was okay. She shivered anew as he wrapped his arms around her. He held her for what seemed like minutes until the shaking finally subsided. Taylor was still a little shaky as he walked her to the hangar where Wade showed her how to re-pack the parachutes to prepare them for the next day's dive.

Wade sent the pilot home, leaving the two of them all alone inside the hangar with nothing around them in that huge open space but mountains of silky parachute fabric smothering the floor around them. She got lost again. She saw herself reach out for him and slowly take his shirt off. She spread soft butterfly kisses all across his big muscular chest; rubbed her fingers over his hardening nipples, and sucked them. It was his turn to shiver as she kissed his stomach and his lower belly. She unzipped his pants and mouthed the fabric of his underwear as his penis hardened through his moistening underwear. Teasing him through his briefs, she gently nibbled on the head of his penis and stroked his balls, working them back and forth with her fingers, slowly and tenderly as his legs twitched beneath her.

The sudden scent of Eternity dissolved her reverie. She realized Wade had gone. Seconds later, she heard him yell from the office asking her if she wanted a beer. She yelled, yes. He returned with two bottles of Corona and they went back to work, folding the rest of the parachutes.

Watching him take a sip of his cold beer, she re-commenced her drift. She saw his naked muscular chest drip with sweat as she peeled off his damp underwear and began sucking on him. She felt her mouth move up and down his penis, listened to him as he moaned in delight, and continued her motions until he came into her mouth, leaving her no other choice but to swallow his warm juices. She saw herself standing before him, slowly unbuttoning her shirt, then taking off her jeans, her T-shirt, her bra, and, finally, her panties. Completely naked, she sat on top of him and placed his penis inside her. Moving up and down on top of him, slowly at first, teasing him, then faster and faster in a frenzy, she began to build into her best orgasm ever. As her prolonged climax drew to a lingering close, the warm liquid saturated him and she collapsed onto his chest and closed her eyes, feeling completely satisfied.

The backfire of a truck brought her back. As she watched it pull up to the hangar, she felt the tell-tale dampness between her legs turn cool, but the throbbing through her jeans remained strong. Meanwhile, Wade had gone to the driver's side of the truck and was talking to him. In her angle of sight, she could see how tightly his jeans fit, and how well they highlighted his incredible ass. She watched him run his hand through his hair and push a few strands away from his face. That little gesture increased her throbbing even more and took her breath away.

She quickly stood up and went outside to get some air.

Never before had she experienced anything quite like this: she had never even touched Wade, yet she could feel him inside her.

When she saw the truck pull away, she went back inside to help him finish cleaning up. They had another beer and talked about the jump, before he walked her back to her car. When she turned to open the car door, she could feel him standing behind her, his scent surrounding her. He put his hand on her shoulder, and leaning towards her, he whispered into her ear: "I would like to see you again, is that possible?

She took in a deep breath and smiled as she whispered her reply: "The possibilities are endless."

Fasten Your Seat Belts

When I first stepped onto the plane, I couldn't help but notice the handsome captain as he stood by the door, welcoming the passengers onboard. He was a tall man, with dark hair and beautiful blue eyes. As I took my seat, my mind was still on him, by then speculating as to how his hands would feel caressing my body. Later, the flight attendant brought me a Bloody Mary. I finished it and dozed off to sleep.

I heard the bathroom door open behind me as I washed my face at the basin. I turned around and saw the captain. He grabbed a hold of my chin and brought his mouth down to mine, his tongue licking across my lips. He kissed my neck and then moved up towards my ear and bit it gently.

I froze and couldn't speak. I was stunned by his presence. He was standing so close to me I could feel the warmth of his breath on my neck. He lifted up my skirt, pulled off my panties and placed his fingers between my legs, fondled me and then withdrew. As if I were the weight of a feather, he lifted me up and sat me on the sink counter. Immediately, he knelt and nuzzled his head between my legs. His tongue moved back and forth quickly, until, moments later, he lifted his face up and moaned: "Oh baby, you taste so good, I could stay down here forever."

He continued licking me, his tongue stabbing in and out of me, assisted most wonderfully by his fingers. I became dizzy, my hands pushing against the walls for support. My ever-moistening body quaked as my heartbeat increased until I experienced the most unbelievable orgasm. Even with my release he continued his actions at an even faster rate, his fingers pulling in and out of me, his tongue frenetic.

The captain got up quickly, unbuckled his pants, and let them drop to the floor.

I saw he wore nothing underneath as my eyes feasted on the largest dick I'd ever seen. It was huge. He wrapped his hand around his hardening cock and began stroking it to full erection. I placed my hand over his, letting him know my intentions, and slipped off the basin and onto my knees before him. I angled his gigantic dick toward my mouth. Realizing I had never experienced anything this large in my mouth before, I worked my lips and tongue around it circumspectly. Instead of trying to take the whole thing in my mouth, I worked my way from the sides to the very tip, licking it, sucking it, pausing to lick and suck on his balls, which I carefully took in my mouth, one-by-one as I massaged the other with my fingers. I sucked on him some more, then put as much of him in my mouth as I could, moving up and down over it until I could feel it grow even larger.

He grabbed me by the hair, pulled me off his dick and up toward him. In one easy motion he turned me toward the mirror, then entered me. I adjusted to the small dimensions of the bathroom by kneeling up onto the sink counter, and bending over to give him just enough room for an easy stroke. He moved inside me with a fierce speed.

Hardly containing my excitement, I started to scream, but heard nothing escape my lips. I reached my hand between my legs and placed my fingers inside alongside his dick enjoying the pleasurable rhythm as I moved in and out along with him. He grabbed my hand and put my fingers to his mouth, sucking on them. He continued to move inside me until he quickly pulled his dick out of me and I felt him spurt his cum all over my ass. He moaned long and satisfied, then pulled me off the sink counter and turned me around to face him. Feeling his cum dripping down my leg exited me – I wanted him again.

I clutched his dick and rubbed it into the moistness between my legs, up and down until I could feel my lips swell with excitement as his dick began to harden. Then I climbed back up onto the sink, wrapped my legs around his back as he reentered me and picked up where he had left off, moving in and out of me quickly, until I came again. He pulled out of me and went down between my legs to drink up the juices that rushed out.

When we were finished, he gently cleaned me off with some paper towels. He picked up my panties from the floor and helped me into them, then smoothed down my skirt before he proceeded to dress. We kissed and he said goodbye. He closed the door behind him. After fixing my hair I went back to my seat.

An hour passed. The flight attendant came to my seat and said the captain wanted to see me in the cockpit. What an appropriate name, I smiled to myself as I walked towards the front of the plane and knocked on the door. It opened. The captain and his co-pilot were smiling as I walked in. Though somewhat startled, I welcomed being in the company of two handsome men. I closed the door behind me and eyed them as I slowly unbuttoned my top.

Before I had two buttons undone, the co-pilot stood up and helped me. After my shirt was off, he pushed my bra to the side of my left breast. He sucked on my nipple, then placed the whole breast in his mouth. I fell back against the door, initially fearful of being overheard, until the pleasure overtook me.

The captain, meanwhile, had lifted my skirt up, pulled my panties off, sunk to his knees, and was now licking me between the legs. The sensation of two men sucking and licking me all over was exhilarating. I had four hands touching my body, pinching, grabbing, entering me, and giving me enormous pleasure. Before too long, I was sprawled atop the control panel, buttons and lights flashing beneath me. I looked dreamily out through the window, the sky and clouds floating below, smiling as I felt that by now familiar hard dick enter me without difficulty.

The co-pilot continued sucking on my breasts, biting and squeezing my nipples until I squirmed in pain. As the captain pushed his dick in and out of me, the copilot positioned himself near my head and put his dick in my mouth. It wasn't as large as the captain's and yet fit perfectly in my mouth. As he moved it in and out of my mouth, his hands remained busy pinching my nipples. I sucked on him, grabbing his balls in my hand and massaging them gently as the captain continued moving in and out of me. All at once we all came

– the captain inside of me, the co-pilot in my mouth, and myself, writhing explosively from the dual efforts of the handsome men. It was the most intense experience I ever had.

When I finally got up, my legs were like rubber, my muscles stiff and sore, my back tender and bruised from the buttons and knobs of the control panel. We dressed quickly and said our good-byes. The co-pilot opened the door for me and closed it behind me as I walked down the aisle towards my seat. The cabin was dark and people slept; I must have been in there for a long time.

After a good night's sleep, I awoke to the sound of the captain's broadcast that we'd be landing within a half hour. As the seatbelt lights went on, the captain added that he hoped we had an enjoyable flight. I felt a little dizzy and sleepy.

As I fastened my seat belt I realized I was wearing jeans, I wasn't wearing a skirt at all – had it all been just a dream?

When I walked off the plane I smiled at the captain and the co-pilot as they waved goodbye. I couldn't help staring at them; I couldn't help wondering what really happened.

I couldn't wait to take another nap.

Bondage Night

Rachel and Kevin's relationship had been deteriorating for some time. They started spending time apart, each doing things with their respective friends, rather than with each other. They were more like roommates now, no longer the couple who had been married for six years. Nevertheless, Rachel kept trying. She tried everything to rekindle the fire, but nothing seemed to work.

One Saturday night Rachel's girlfriends planned a "night out with the girls." They would all meet at Stacie's house. Each of them would bring a bottle of wine, a food dish, and a story of a sexual experience to share with the group. Rachel found this difficult since Kevin was the only man she had ever been with. Plus, as of late their sex life was minimal at best.

As the night progressed and the wine flowed, the stories of sexual experiences became more and more detailed and graphic. Rachel's friend, Kara, told of a night she had met a married man at a bar and had sex with him in the men's bathroom. Katherine told the story of how she and a girlfriend met two guys, while out dancing one night, had followed them to their house and ended up in a foursome. She added that when she had woken up she was a little embarrassed, slightly sore, but incredibly excited, and giggled all the way home.

Tiffanie's story, told with the greatest of drama, was the best though. She told how she had given her boyfriend a blowjob in a taxi on their way to the airport, then continued their antics once they were on the plane. Once seated and covered with a blanket, Tiffanie sat on her boyfriend's lap. He entered her and the two had sex right there on the plane.

When it came Rachel's turn, she decided to just make something up.

She told how one night Kevin came home from work tired and complaining of an aching back. She made him take off his shirt and lay down on the floor. She brought out some oil, poured it on his back and begun to massage him. As she rubbed the oil onto his skin and moved her hands over his smooth back, she felt herself getting excited. Then, as she reached his shoulders, Kevin moaned. That started to get her wet and tingly between her legs. She continued rubbing him and asked him to turn over so she could rub his chest and stomach. Once Kevin was on his back, Rachel had pulled off his pants and rubbed his penis through the fabric of his underwear. Noticing the dampness begin to spread across the front of them. An idea had occurred to her.

She asked him if he was willing to try something new, if he wanted to experiment. He told her to do whatever she wanted. Smiling deviously at what only she knew lay in store, she went to the other room and returned with a handful of items.

Back on the floor she took the first item, a silk scarf, and wrapped it around his eyes, blindfolding him. Then she secured his wrists tightly to the leg of the coffee table with another scarf, immobilizing him. After a few moments she took a cube of ice from a bowl and carefully touched just the tip of it on his right nipple. As his body twitched, she ran the ice cube across his chest and down to his stomach. As Kevin twitched uncontrollably, she ran the ice cube over the fabric of his underwear, breathing heavily at the sounds of his moans and his begging her to stop.

Rachel pulled his underwear off and began sucking on his penis, carefully cupping his balls in her hand and playfully rolling them through her fingers. When she felt Kevin about to come, she sucked on him harder and faster, allowing him to come in her mouth. A couple minutes later, after restoring his full erection, she then sat atop of him and guided his hard-as-a-rock penis inside of her. She moved her body up and down on top of him, pinching his nipples, fondling his balls – all at the same time.

She felt his body flinch beneath her as she rode him like a bronco – completely out of control – holding on for dear life and loving every minute of it. They came simultaneously, their bodies instantly exhausted. Her sweat dripped off her forehead onto his chest and rolled across his nipple that she fingered and wiped at, causing him to flinch some more.

Exhausted and totally spent, she climbed off of him and lay down next to him on the floor. Once she had untied his wrists from the coffee table and taken the scarf off his eyes, he rolled over to face her, looked into her eyes, and said how amazing the experience had been. He thanked her and kissed her softly.

As Rachel looked around the room, she could tell the girls had been affected by the story. She told them it was this particular evening that helped to save her marriage. In fact, she added, she had to leave early tonight. Kevin and her had plans to drip honey onto their bodies and lick it off.

As the others continued telling stories, Rachel could no longer concentrate. Her mind was on Kevin and finding a way to make their marriage work. Perhaps a night of uninhibited sex would do them good. After saying her goodbyes, she quickly left and headed home.

When she got home she told Kevin about the evening with the girls and shared the story she'd made up. As she told it, she could see him getting excited. The bulge in his pants started to grow, as did the stain spreading across his lap. He took a hold of her hand and led her into their bedroom.

That night they made love for hours. They tried new positions, talked about their fantasies and explored each other's bodies until they were thoroughly exhausted.

Their marriage did get better; they just celebrated their ten-year anniversary. Every Wednesday the girls have a "theme" night; the first of which was Rachel's "bondage night." As for Kevin, every time Rachel wants to go out with the girls, Kevin says "go for it".

Sleeping On the Job

He came up behind her as she sat at her desk and started massaging her neck and shoulders. Then, very carefully, his hands slipped down to her breasts and lingered. For a while, he rubbed his fingers across her nipples, playfully squeezing them. He then grabbed her breasts and ran his fingers up and down across her nipples, until they hardened. He brought his hands back up towards her neck and massaged her again. Meanwhile, she sat silently, craving more, but unsure how to communicate it.

Slowly, he spun her chair around until she faced him and went to his knees. He pushed her skirt up past her thighs. He took her heels off and reverently placed them on the floor. He slid his warm hand up inside her skirt to the top of her pantyhose and pulled them down around her hips, hesitated briefly, then continued his motion down her thighs to her toes, until they were off. He reached up inside her skirt, smiling, apparently happy to find she wore no panties. His hands trembled and she could almost feel his pulse race. Pushing the skirt a little higher, he put his face into her lap between her legs. He started licking her, slowly at first, but soon moving a little faster, building as he dug his tongue into her as far as it could go.

Vaguely uncomfortable in the sitting position through all the pleasure, she shifted, bracing herself on the armrests, squirming up and down, unable to sit still. She moaned, quietly at first, until all of a sudden she crescendoed with a scream. He was driving her crazy; it felt so good she wanted more.

Minutes later, she felt release, a gush of liquid squirting out over his face, her body shivering one last time before going limp. She looked down at him, and saw him licking his lips, clearly enjoying himself while licking up the juices he had caused to flow from her body. He reached behind her to unbutton her skirt and pulled it off, revealing her nakedness. Carefully, he undid the hook at the back of her bra, slid the straps off her shoulders and threw the bra to the floor.

She was motionless as his admiring eyes traveled over her body. He complemented her round firm breasts and her perfectly erect nipples. He bent his mouth to her right breast and sucked while his hand found her left and gently massaged. He moved back and forth from one breast to the other sucking, squeezing and tenderly biting.

Impatiently and out of control, she stood up, grabbed a hold of his shoulders and pushed him down on to the floor. Quickly, urgently, deftly she pulled his pants off and her fingers found the hem of his briefs, yanked them down and her eyes lit on his hard and throbbing dick. She clutched it with one hand, wrapped her lips around it, and began licking it. Then taking the whole thing in her mouth, she moved her mouth up and down, over and over again, until he lost control himself, moaning and screaming, and his body slithered and jumped around on the floor like a reeled in fish. She kept sucking on him until he finally came, keeping her mouth over him, swallowing his juices as they shot into her mouth.

As he lay there panting, she once again grabbed a hold of his dick and rubbed her hand up and down his shaft until it sprung back into action. Then she climbed atop him, centered her moistness directly over his dick, and guided him into her. She moved up and down, feeling his hardness. Moments later, just as she felt him on the verge of coming, she pulled off him abruptly. She told him to enter her from behind.

She went down on her hands and knees as he positioned himself behind her. He carefully entered her. In and out, he pumped hard against her bare ass. She screamed for more as he moved faster and faster, in and out. All of a sudden, she felt his body jerk as he came inside her. They both dropped onto the floor; him lying on top of her, and together they came in a flood of warmth.

All of a sudden she felt someone tapping her on the shoulder, "Tanya wake up... Tanya..." the voice said before drifting off. She awoke fully.

She lifted her head slowly from her desk and gazed through the glass into the conference room. Then she felt the cool air of the ventilation system on her breasts and gazed down and saw the top button of her blouse undone. She looked around apprehensively as she buttoned it back up discretely. Inside the large inner office was the man she had noticed earlier, the man who had quickly become the object of her afternoon fantasy. Only a few feet away from her, he was still involved in a heavy meeting with one of the partners through the glassed-in walls of the conference room. She couldn't help but stare at him. She wanted to get his attention, so she went to the ladies room and took off her panties.

Once she had sat back down at her desk, she turned in her chair so her lap faced in his direction. Seconds later he turned and his eyes shot in her direction. She opened her legs. At first he seemed startled... did a double take, continued to look, and still managed to finish his meeting.

After the meeting, he came out of the conference room and, in passing, put his business card onto the desk in front of her. "I'd really like it if you'd call me. I have a feeling I've got something you want."

Then he smiled and walked off toward the elevator.

Could the real thing be as good as the fantasy? She doubted it as she tossed the card into the wastebasket. She placed her fingers between her legs, playing with herself and contemplating her next fantasy. Who would it be? The water boy? The office supplies deliveryman? Or maybe the man who had just started work in the office next to her?

That's the nice thing about fantasies – they can be about anyone doing anything you want.

Special Secrets

The girls arrived in Vegas at about four in the afternoon. The weather was unbearably hot, but the drinks were refreshingly cold. They had booked two rooms. Kara and Stephanie planned to share one, while Lindsey and Tanya, arriving tomorrow, would take the other.

They anticipated the coming weekend as a great adventure – a time none of them would ever forget and this meant of course that no one back home would ever hear about it.

Once they unpacked their bags, leaving the room in total disarray, they finished the complimentary bottle of champagne and then the girls set off on their mission. Downstairs they gambled a little and drank way too much, before heading for the "Olympic Gardens," a nearby strip joint. By then both girls decided they wanted a lap dance by a female dancer.

When they got to the club, they ordered drinks and began eyeing the dancers. After a bit they chose their dancers. Kara picked a beautiful blonde dancer with very large breasts and Stephanie chose a tall brunette.

The excitement seemed mutual, which only added to the adventure. The dancers seemed to appreciate the girls they danced for as much as Kara and Stephanie enjoyed their dances. During the dance, the blonde dancer stuck her breasts in Kara's face and swept her nipples across her mouth and pressed. Kara's head was forced back against the chair, but her eyes never left the dancer. Then the blonde dancer took Kara's hands and guided them across her chest allowing her to caress her breasts. Kara brought her mouth towards it, sucking on one nipple very gently.

Nearby, Stephanie's hands touched the firm ass of her dancer, bringing her closer, until their lips touched in a kiss. The experience awakened feelings in Stephanie that, although ever curious, had never pursued. And it seemed mutual for the brunette. It was incredible and sexy and something that every woman should try at least once in her lifetime, Kara thought.

When Kara and Stephanie returned to their room, they were drunk with excitement and curiosity – and way too much champagne. They decided to take a bubble bath together, both of them wondering what might happen, but neither saying a thing.

Covered in bubbles, Stephanie started giving Kara a massage, her hands gently touching her friend's neck, back, and bottom. Suddenly, she reached around and started to massage Kara's breasts. Kara sat for a moment until she seemed to realize what was happening and turned and faced Stephanie. They kissed – tenderly at first – but then the kisses became rough in mounting arousal as their hands traveled everywhere on each others' bodies. They got out of the bathtub, naked and dripping bubbles on the carpet, they walked into the bedroom, where they sat on the bed and continued kissing.

Kara leaned back against the fluffy pillows. Stephanie kissed her breasts, sucked her nipples, playing with them between her fingers, as she pleased Kara in ways that Stephanie knew her friend would enjoy. Stephanie placed the fingers of her other hand between Kara's legs and then slid down there and started kissing her. Stephanie licked down there and played until finally Kara asked if she could return the favor. Stephanie happily took Kara up on her offer. In tune with each other, both women knew what the other would enjoy. Their lovemaking was exciting, powerful, tender, yet rough and unbelievably enjoyable.

At one point Stephanie brought out a large vibrator, still wrapped in its package, and confessed her hopes that this was where their evening would lead. Kara said she had felt the same way.

They discovered that over the years they both had been curious about what it would be like to be with another female, but neither had ever had the opportunity until now. The female body is such a beautiful thing, Kara remarked, that only another female could ever really know exactly what we feel or how we want to feel.

The two played with the toy for hours, taking turns moving it in and out of one another, watching as they made each other squirm with pleasure. They kissed and they touched. Finally, after they had fully explored each other's bodies, they fell asleep entwined together, dozing off fully content.

The next morning brought no weird feelings or discomfort. Everything was exactly how it should be. The two friends were closer now than ever; they had shared an experience almost every woman considers at least once in her lifetime.

Later on that morning, when the other girls showed up, Lindsey asked cheerfully: "You guys ready to begin our adventure?"

Kara and Stephanie just smiled at each other, and Kara said, "Let's go."

It was a memorable weekend and a true adventure – theirs to share.

Jasmine

My secretary walked into my office as she did every day, delivering my messages. She wore a red silk shirt, unbuttoned just low enough to allow her incredibly full breasts to announce themselves and invite me in. I tried concentrating on what she was saying, but couldn't help wondering what they would taste like. As she left the office, I watched her perfectly round ass swish from side to side and I could feel the bulge in my pants start to grow as ripples of shivers went through my body. She had this effect on me every time she came near.

One day, when I walked out to bring her a document that needed typing, I found her bent over a drawer of the file cabinet, her ass up in the air. I had to restrain myself from tearing my pants off and entering her. She turned around suddenly and faced me. My heartbeat quickened, I wiped the beads of perspiration off my forehead as I handed her the document. My hands trembling slightly. She asked me how soon I needed it and I told her I wanted it as soon as possible. We both smiled at the unspoken. I was afraid of what actions I might take if I stood there too long, so I turned around and walked back into my office. Closing the door behind me, I spent the next hour fantasizing about what an evening with her might be like.

I would show up about seven to pick her up for dinner. She would invite me in and we would have a glass of wine.

Her small apartment was decorated with her distinctly feminine touch. A vase with freshly cut flowers stood on the table and candles were lit around the room. The soft sound of jazz played on the stereo and a hint of jasmine floated around me.

The aroma mesmerized me, sweeping me off to a place I had often longed for. She excused herself as she went into her bathroom, only to come out wearing nothing but lace underwear and a matching bra. She sauntered over to where I sat on the couch and sat down in my lap, straddling me like the studhorse I always imagined myself to be. She leaned up close to me, placing my face between her breasts, and begged me to touch them. I grabbed hold of one, coaxed it out from its' snug little place inside her bra, touched the nipple with my tongue, then placed it in my mouth.

She tightened her legs around me, the quickness of her breathing increasing. I continued sucking on her breast while letting the other out to play. She reached behind her back, unhooked her bra, and allowed her unbelievable breasts to flow beautifully in front of me. As I played with her breasts, squeezing them hard and pinching her nipples, she unzipped my pants and brought out my penis.

She sidled down my body and starting sucking on it, giving me the best blowjob I'd ever had. Feeling her mouth on my balls in her mouth, taking them in, I twitched from the painful pleasure. My embarrassment about coming so quickly didn't faze her as she stood up to remove her panties. I was pleased to see she was completely shaved and found myself hardening once again and eager to get inside her. She laid down on the couch next to me begging for me to go down on her. I happily complied.

She tasted so sweet as I moved my tongue inside the tight little space of which I had dreamed for so long. She screamed my name out loud and showed obvious signs of pleasure, begging me to continue. Pulling me up towards her, she grabbed hold of my penis, forcing it inside her. Her wetness and incredible tightness excited me to total combustion. I came in a flood, a wild river completely out of control.

We lay together on the couch completely exhausted and totally content ... both pleased by the most amazing sex either of us had ever had.

I was startled out of my reverie by the knock on my door.

"Mr. Peterson, I've finished the typing," she smiled as she peeked in and entered. She handed me the file. "It's almost five. Would you mind if I left a little early? My boyfriend's picking me up to take me to dinner."

I excused her and watched as she walked away, afraid to get up for fear she'd notice the bulge in my pants and the stain that had spread across my lap. When I was sure that she had left the office, I went to the window to watch her walk outside.

I saw as her boyfriend got out of a car parked in front and walk around to open the door for her. They hugged and kissed passionately, her beautiful arms wrapped tightly around his body. I knew exactly what they were going to be doing that night; he was a very lucky guy!

That One Incredible Evening

The newspaper ad read:

"When I close my eyes, I can picture your face and it brings back the memory of that evening; that one incredible evening filled with the most amazingly wonderful feelings a woman could ever experience. Do you remember me the way that I remember you? Was it as amazing for you? I never asked for your number, you never asked for mine, but I desperately want to see you again, to touch you again. I know your name is Kyle, I know your lips are soft and your hands are warm. My name is Chloe and we met on the beach at sunset. If you'd like to see me again, please call me at 777-1234."

It took all her courage to place the ad in the local paper, but the memory of him was so incredible that every day that followed made his touch seem more overpowering than it was on that wonderful evening. So crazy and unpredictable, it took Chloe completely by surprise at a time when she felt at her lowest. Tommy had cheated on her again ... what a surprise! Only this time it had been with her best friend and apparently everyone knew it but Chloe.

It started on her friend Susan's birthday. Chloe spent the whole day preparing for it – shopping, decorating, and cooking. She had bought Susan this great dress and thought she'd take it over to her in case she wanted to wear it that night. At her door she knocked and the door slowly opened. Chloe stepped in and walked through the house, looking around for Susan. Then came the shock with the full picture of where her friend was...and with whom.

She found Susan and her Tommy outside on the hammock, naked, and making love in a way she didn't remember ever sharing with Tommy. Chloe backed away from the window and quickly jotted down a note: "Susan, the party has been canceled... enjoy the dress."

Chloe then dragged herself from Susan's place with a chaos of feelings: a potent mixture of emptiness, betrayal and relief. She and Tommy really hadn't been together very long and although she enjoyed spending time with him, she admitted "that feeling" was never there. She knew the feeling well, but only from afar: the one when he walks into the room your heart slowly sinks to the floor and you are afraid to bend down and pick it up for fear of falling over? When you are not with him, you almost feel like a piece of your body is missing, but you don't realize it until he's back and you feel complete; as if the piece has been returned to you.

Truth was, Chloe had never experienced that feeling firsthand. She just imagined what it would be like and knew until she felt it, whatever relationship she was in, it was not "the true relationship."

Until that night.

On her way home, Chloe decided to pick up a bottle of wine, a cheap bottle opener, and a pack of cigarettes, although she didn't even smoke. The guy at the cash register threw in a couple of glasses for free. She walked down to the beach and sat on a gnarly old piece of driftwood, its rough scars from the sea very much in evidence. She opened the bottle of wine, poured herself a glass, and stared out at the sea, reflecting on the day's events.

After an hour and two glasses of wine later, a man walked down the steps of one of the houses on the beach. Chloe watched him as he crossed the sand to the water. He was tall with dark hair and matching mustache and goatee. He was wearing white drawstring pants, rolled up at the cuffs, and a sweater draped over his shoulders. But his chest was bare and she could see how solid it was. He was beautiful. As he crossed, his eyes lit on Chloe, and shortly after he began drifting off course in her direction. As she determined his intent, Chloe felt her skin moisten and her heart beat faster. As he neared her, he smiled, introduced himself, and asked if she'd mind if he sat down with her. He introduced himself as Kyle. In the next twenty minutes they were talking and laughing. And all out of wine.

Pointing back to the houses along the beach, he suggested she come and sit on his deck with him to watch the sunset, promising her a cold glass of wine, or three. She assented.

As they stood to walk up, she noticed he was taller than she originally thought. She had already noticed his teal colored eyes with eyelashes that went on forever.

Back at his beachfront home, they walked up a flight of steps to his deck and she sat while he went inside. Along the rail she noticed hundreds of shells. When he came back with some wine, she asked about the shells. He explained that whenever he traveled he would collect shells from the beaches and bring them home; they were from all over the world.

As the sun crept down toward the horizon he shared many stories with her and they continued to laugh and enjoy each other's company. As the sun finally found its resting place, they found their's in each other's arms in a hug that could have lasted forever, both of them holding on for dear life, neither seeming to want it to end.

Chloe looked up at him and he slowly bent his mouth close to hers. As if in some kind of magical dream, they touched and for just that very second, they became one. His lips were so soft, his kiss so gentle. He pulled away from her, took her hand and walked her over to an old overstuffed couch that stood on the deck.

He unbuttoned her blouse, kissing her neck, her chest, and slowly he took her shirt off. He unhooked her bra, and as he slid the straps off her shoulders, he kissed them, softly looking into her eyes after each kiss. He kissed her neck again, behind her ears, along the shoulders, and slowly made his way down to her breasts taking a nipple into his mouth, biting it with a tender kind of roughness that sent shivers down her spine. She rubbed her hands across his chest, massaging his shoulders and arms. She trailed one finger down to his lower stomach where she slowly untied the drawstring of his pants and helped him out of them. He wore nothing underneath and she discovered a perfectly sized penis that she longed to touch.

Although Chloe did not have much sexual experience, the next hour came naturally to her. She not only knew exactly how to please him; but she *wanted* to please him. For a long while, they lay down together on the couch and discovered each other's bodies, tenderly caressing, kissing, and intimately exploring. Kyle kissed her stomach and the inside of her thighs, and then slowly took his tongue down between her legs where he brought her to heights of passion she completely surrendered to.

After what seemed like hours, Kyle came up to kiss her. She could feel his erect penis pushing against her, as if screaming to come inside. Chloe took her hand and carefully grabbed a hold of it. Gently massaging his balls, she brought her mouth down around it, kissing and sucking, feeling his body squirm next to hers. He moaned and she smiled. The more he moaned, the more she sought to please him. She took her mouth off his penis, and teasingly licked the tip and the sides. Then she climbed on top of him, and escorted him into her. For an interminable second, they sat frozen.

She let him enter her further and then she slowly moved up and down, back and forth, feeling him inside her and enjoying every second. They moved together, slowly at first, then faster, then harder by degrees, until beads of sweat dripped onto Kyle's chest, and at that very second they both came together and screamed with joyous pleasure. Chloe, exhausted, lay down on top of Kyle, feeling his rapid heartbeat.

The next thing she knew the sun was peeking through windows off the porch. She was alone on the couch, wrapped in an old patchwork quilt. She looked around, but Kyle wasn't anywhere to be seen. She saw a note on the table, picked it up and read. It said: "Thank you, it was beautiful and so are you – Kyle."

That was it. She got dressed and walked down the steps back onto the sand, along the beach, to the street, where she got in her car and drove back to her apartment. The answering machine was blinking; she turned it on to six, "I'm sorry," messages from Tommy, one from Susan, and the dry cleaning was ready to pick up.

Chloe took a shower, made some coffee, and sat at the kitchen table, wondering if what had happened had only been a dream or not. Kyle was gone. The night had been passionate and amazing. Then over, just like that.

Who was this guy? Was he married? How the hell was she supposed to see him again? They hadn't exchanged numbers. Would she ever hear from him again?

Later that day Chloe returned to the beach house. She summoned the courage to knock on the door, but no one answered. She peeked into the windows and saw the place looked empty. A neighbor saw her, came over and told her the guy who had been staying there was gone, and added that he didn't have a phone and probably wouldn't be back.

He told her that the house had been on the market and had sold recently, so, he said, his neighbor, Kyle must have stayed there one last weekend. No one knew where he'd gone or how to reach him.

Chloe walked down the beach feeling lonelier and emptier than she had when she first had walked onto the beach the day before, before Kyle had walked into her life, then vanished.

A few weeks later, Chloe still couldn't get Kyle out of her head. In the meantime, she and Susan had made up, after Chloe discovered

Tommy was out of the picture completely. Chloe then confessed her evening and expressed her heartbreak. It was Susan's idea to place a personal ad in the local newspaper.

Within a week Susan brought the paper to Chloe and showed her a response to her ad:

> *"Hi Chloe. Yes, it was a wonderful night and you are a beautiful woman. You touched my heart in ways I have never felt, but I am married to a woman who is terminally ill, and I need to be by her side until the end. That evening with you was selfish on my part, though I haven't made love in over ten years. But when I met you, I felt this need to be touched by you. I am so sorry to have been dishonest with you. Thank you, again, for what will be my most cherished memory. Kyle."*

It took Chloe a long time to get over the news and to understand where Kyle was coming from until finally, she could enjoy the evening for what it was. A once-in-a-lifetime moment with "that feeling," where your heart skips a beat, and for just one instant you feel a connection with someone who makes you feel like you are the only woman on earth, that you are his everything.

Especially that you really can rock someone's world ... he had certainly rocked hers.

And They Finally Met...

He was the kindest, sweetest, most romantic man Victoria had never met. And the most incredibly handsome she was sure. He was a friend of a friend and they had only ever talked on the phone. The occasion was one of their "girl's night" out evenings. Victoria and her girlfriend were drinking and being silly. At 2:00 a.m. they decided to call people. Victoria's friend couldn't reach her boyfriend, so she called his best friend, Kurt, instead. They started talking.

Before too long, Victoria took over the phone and started flirting with Kurt, a complete stranger. Even so, his charm, personality and a certain spirituality came through and touched her deeply. After that night, the first phone call turned into another, and another. It soon turned into a ritual for them to call Kurt every time the girls were out together. He lived in Denver, they in California. Consequently Kurt was usually sound asleep when they called, but he never seemed too tired to talk.

Eventually, Victoria called him on her own and a kind of friendship began to build with each subsequent phone call, one in which they were getting to know one another, but neither getting too close or personal. After a while, the conversations turned into e-mails. They wrote back and forth for a while until Kurt's interest seemed to fade. So Victoria stopped writing.

But one day came a happy accident. Victoria inadvertently sent

Kurt an e-mail, to which he quickly responded, and the correspondence began anew. Only this time, their communication seemed more meaningful. Both took the time to express their thoughts, beliefs and interests. Their friendship went from silly and mildly sexual, to honest and deep. She shared her dreams with Kurt and he encouraged her in all of them. For his part, he opened up to her, brought her into his life and into his heart, trusting her with things that mattered.

As the e-mails continued, their friendship deepened, neither knowing where it was going or what would happen when it got there. Sexual innuendoes ran throughout the content of their e-mails, and these eventually brought them round to conversations about making love. They talked about what each liked and what they would like to try and found that their interests were similar. They also found that these conversations led to the mutual thought that both would like to eventually try these things with the other.

The e-mails turned back into phone conversations and their friendship began to blossom into what both hoped would be a future together. Neither knew what the other looked liked, but each fell in love with whom the other was inside. They planned a date to meet, of which both confessed understandable nervousness and excitement to the other. Both of their lives had been deeply touched and hurt by love; both were nevertheless encouraged with the prospect of finding it again; but both were scared and self-protective.

The day of their meeting arrived. Victoria spent the day getting her hair and nails done, cleaning her house, and running in and out of the bathroom, as she was nauseous from her nervousness.

Kurt was long past the worried stage. He was now concentrated on the possibility of this meeting leading to everything he had ever dreamed of, yet prepared himself for it being everything he feared.

Finally his plane touched down in California. Kurt, placing his feet firmly on the ground of her territory, rented a car and headed to her house. The drive, though short, seemed to take forever.

The doorbell rang and Victoria felt her stomach turn. She would finally meet the man who had brightened her days and finally made her smile again. She opened the door. Standing there was the man she had pictured, exactly – the kindest man she ever knew. He smiled at her, handed her a bouquet of flowers, and hugged her. The prolonged hug didn't end – they just stood in the doorway holding each other and thanking everything above for bringing them together and for making this moment happen. They stared at each other, absorbing the moment, neither making the first move. Then they kissed – a warm, passionate, lovely kiss. When they pulled apart, she took his hand and led him inside.

Every candle in the house was burning and Victoria had champagne on ice. Luther Vandross sang in the background. Kurt took her hand, brought her close to him and held her. They had finally come together and they were happy. They danced and drank champagne and danced some more. They talked and laughed and told each other about their pent-up nervousness over their first meeting and laughed as it dissolved in the subdued flickers of candlelight.

Not long after, Victoria led Kurt upstairs to her bedroom where they stood together in the light of two candles, staring at one another; not wanting to go too fast for fear of not enjoying every single second they would have together. She reached out towards him and helped him take his shirt off; he did the same for her. Together they undressed, slowly without any awkwardness. They sat down on her bed and he touched her; ran his hand down her arm and then brought it back, touching her face. Kurt looked into her eyes and told her how beautiful she was to him and she cried. She had heard these words before, but never had they meant as much as now. They kissed and touched one another; they fell in love and then they made love. It was never one doing something for the other, it was them doing everything together. Each was unselfish, each eager to please the other.

When they woke up with their bodies entwined, neither wanted to let go. For an hour, each feigned sleep not aware the other was awake. Victoria finally pulled her arm out from under him. He opened his eyes and saw that she was watching him. She smiled. They kissed and made love again, this time more passionately and creatively, with newfound knowledge. She had the most incredible orgasm – or three – that she had ever reached. By the smile on his face, she could tell he felt the same.

They got up, showered, and made plans to spend the day at the beach. They hadn't eaten the night before, so they made breakfast together. Although she tried to put up a fight, they watched a little football. The weather was beautiful, the ocean water wasn't too cold and their hands never let go. They walked the beach, went for lunch, and spent the rest of the day getting to know each other.

It was romantic; it was the best day of their lives.

Then Victoria heard the doorbell ring for the second time that day:

He's here.

It's Never Too Late
To Say "I Love You"

Every time she looked at him, her heart would beat, her skin would dampen, her face would redden. It was amazing to her how one man could so easily crumble down the walls of self-control she had worked so hard to erect.

They had met accidentally – or maybe it was fate, who knows? He was standing up on a scaffold at a job site next to her office building where one lunchtime she decided to soak up some sun in a lawn chair in a parking space outside the office. He was an electrician, she was a secretary; two people from two different worlds. From above her he mentioned how nice a cold bottle of Chardonnay would be and she replied questioning when he would be pouring it.

Every day after that they would make sure to bump into one another, and mention that bottle of wine. She would ask when he was going to bring in some wine for her and he would always reply "when you bring in some for me." So one day she brought in a cold bottle of Clos Du Bois Chardonnay, wrapped in a wine gift bag. She tied it to the side mirror of his truck with a note wishing him a wonderful weekend, and telling him to enjoy the wine. She signed her name, Katherine, under which she scrawled her telephone number.

When he got off work, he called her, and said, "Hello, this is

Max." He thanked her for the wine and talked about his plans for the weekend. This was their introduction.

The days that followed were filled with smiles, flirtatious comments and vague allusions to Max's reciprocal present to Katherine. This continued for quite some time, until finally Katherine summoned the nerve to ask Max to join her and some friends for a concert in the park. He agreed and they had their first "date" that night.

They lay on a blanket under the stars while the music played for hours in the background. Katherine's friends might as well have been absent, which they soon were. She and Max talked and talked about everything that mattered and some things that didn't.

They stole little kisses from one another throughout the evening. When Katherine spilled her wine all over her hands, Max licked it off her fingers. She said it was lucky that she hadn't spilled any on her stomach, and smiled. He dipped his fingers in the wine, dripped it on her stomach and then licked it off. The kisses were magical and the feelings were scary, but Katherine soaked up every minute of their time together lest it was the last time.

After that night, Max would come to her office and they would have lunch together, but a second date was never mentioned again. He flirted with her and made her nervous, but he also made her laugh and feel pretty. She cherished these weeks as the nicest period of time she had had in some time. She knew his time here was coming to a close, that his job next door was almost finished and that he would soon be gone.

Finally, that day did come, his last day on the job. He would be leaving at 3:30; she sadly watched the clock as it ticked closer to that time. She flirted with him in the lunch line when she ran into him at the deli, and she mentioned that she'd miss him when he went. But he never said a thing, just flirted back. At 3:30, he came in to say goodbye. It was sad for her because she knew she would never see him again. He told her how great it was to meet her, and mentioned what a great time he had at the concert and that he'd give her a call sometime. He never did.

One day, many years later, she was driving down the freeway when a guy raced past her on a Harley. She couldn't make out his features, but something inside told her it was Max, so she followed him. She saw the Harley pull off the freeway and into a nearby market. Katherine pulled up to the market and watched the rider get off his bike, take off his helmet and jacket, and head into the store. Those old feelings rushed inside her, and she was sick with excitement. She was uncertain whether to follow him inside. Finally, she decided to go in since this would be her last chance to see Max again. She checked herself out in the rearview mirror, fixed her hair and walked straight into the market.

Katherine looked all over the store for the mysterious biker; up the bread isle, down the canned food isle and over by the fruits and vegetables, but she couldn't find him. She was puzzled and worried thinking perhaps he went out a different door or that it hadn't been him at all. All of a sudden a cold bottle of Clos Du Bois Chardonnay appeared from over her shoulder.

She turned around and there was Max, as handsome as ever.

He looked into her eyes and said, "I saw you on the freeway, I hoped you'd follow me, but wasn't sure you would. I'm glad you did, it's been a long time."

They talked for a while about what each of them had been up to and how they'd been. There was no mention that Max had never called her. She was curious, but now it didn't matter. They decided to meet for dinner the following evening and both drove off in different directions.

It occurred to Katherine that she might never see him again. But she put that thought out of her mind as she sped home in anticipation of the impending evening.

The following day after work, she poured herself a chamomile bath in hopes to relieve some of the anxieties that brewed inside her. After her long bath, she put on jeans and a cute little top that showed off her well-toned body, and then fixed her hair. Not wanting to appear too eager, she went light on the make up and set out for her night with Max.

The day before they had agreed on meeting at Rosati's, where they'd once met for a beer, and when she pulled up she saw his bike parked out front. Her heart was racing, her stomach churned and she got out of her car trembling slightly on rubbery legs.

What was she scared of? She finally admitted to herself that this man affected her in a way no other man had and now she was having a second opportunity with him – and she wasn't quite sure how to handle it. When she walked in, he called out at her and she walked over. He immediately stood up and looked right in her eyes. It was simple; she knew exactly what she must do. She kissed him, slowly and passionately. This disarmed him, surprised him, but it was obvious he enjoyed it.

After they sat down and ordered dinner, they picked back up on their former characteristic never-ending conversation, talking about everything. At last, Max explained why he never called her: that he felt they were just way too different and it could never work out. He knew she dated sophisticated men with money and he thought maybe she'd be better off without the likes of him. Katherine explained he was the first real man she had met, and it was only with a man like him that she could so easily fall in love. She told him how she wanted to cry one day when he was talking about his Mom and Dad "back home," how he missed them. She confessed to him how much she admired him for being so strong and independent and for doing whatever made him happy. She admitted that she was a little frightened by him but that it was that fear that excited her. He said he thought about her a lot over the years and truly regretted never contacting her.

They had a few beers and way too much conversation and decided to go back to her place. When they got there, she poured a glass of wine for each of them while he built a fire. She spilled a little of the wine on her fingers and he licked them off. He then put his hand under her chin and tilted her lips towards his. He kissed her gently on the lips, then on her cheek and on her eyes. They held each other for a long while, and then he slowly unbuttoned her shirt and started kissing her neck… her chest and her stomach.

They made love in front of the fire. He wrapped his arms around her and they slept as the fire slowly burnt out.

The next morning when Katherine awoke, Max was busy making breakfast. He paused to bring her a cup of coffee. She decided not to mince words and asked him straight out if they would ever see each other again. He explained he had longstanding plans to go on a bike run with some of his buddies and he would be gone for a month. He added that he really couldn't back out of it, nor did he want to. Katherine said she understood, but deep down inside, she felt sad and somewhat rejected. He assured her that, when the ride was over, he would come back to her.

A month went by and she didn't hear from him. Finally, after some months, she received a letter and a package from a stranger who turned out by the letter inside to be Max's Mother. Max had been killed on the ride and his mother had been searching for Katherine for the past six months. She sent Katherine his leather jacket with a letter that Max must have written while out on the ride, but never had sent.

It read:

> *"Dear Katherine: Did I tell you how wonderful it was to be with you again? Did I tell you how beautiful you are and how you fill my heart with love? I can't wait to come back home and into your arms. Please wait for me, I will be back this time I promise. Is it too soon to say I love you? Love Max."*

All that Katherine could whisper was, "I love you too, Max".

Love Letters

The park bench seemed the only place Fiona could be alone these days, her safe and quiet place. She needed this spot; she wasn't happy anymore and didn't know what to do about it. She had married Todd seven years ago at a tender age, but so young that they weren't sure of their mutual love. She had loved him so much and would have done anything for him. They talked for hours about everything and were the best of friends.

But that was then, Fiona thought, an eternity ago. Now they didn't talk much. When had it all begun to fall apart, she asked herself rhetorically. Fiona knew. Two years ago she was told she couldn't have children. Todd wanted a family, a big family like his own. His Mom and Dad had eight kids most of who were married with kids of their own – except for Todd. And, of course, that was Fiona's fault – or so he made her feel.

Since that diagnosis, Todd had pulled away from her. He stayed later at the office and would fall asleep on the couch after watching TV late into the evenings. Fiona had meanwhile fallen into a depression. Especially when she sat here, as she did every day, to watch the duck families play in the water and all the wonderfully happy young couples picnicking on the lawn or sneaking kisses behind a tree. This all made Fiona sad.

On one such day, while sitting on the bench, an older woman

came and sat with her. She introduced herself as Angela, and soon she spoke to Fiona as if lifelong friends. She told Fiona all about her life and loves and shared with her new young friend her years and years of memories.

One story stuck in Fiona's mind and set her thinking. Angela told her about her marriage to an abusive husband, when she was younger. The abuse wasn't physical, she said, but verbal. He would tell her she was no good; that she wasn't worth anything to him or anyone else. This litany of abuse took root in Angela and depressed her until finally she confronted her husband. She told him that she couldn't take it anymore, that she worked so hard to make him happy and to give him everything he wished for, but he was never happy and she had decided to leave. This, Angela said, was not what he wanted to hear. But rather than getting mad, he sat down with her and asked what he could do to make her happy and to convince her to stay with him. Angela explained to him that she loved him very much, but he made her feel bad inside and unappreciated and certainly not loved. From that moment on, their love grew and they started communicating. They fell back in love.

Angela's story inspired Fiona. That very day she went home and called a local florist. She ordered flowers over the phone for Todd. When they came, she wrote on the attached card: "For my dear husband, I love you, I've always loved you, and I miss you. Please come home to me."

Then Fiona rummaged through her sexy nightgowns and pulled out the one she had worn on their honeymoon. It was sheer and lacy, short and sexy, and cream-colored with tiny pearls sewed into the collar, with matching cream-colored panties. Fiona ran to the store and bought more flowers, candles, champagne, and strawberries that she planned to dip into chocolate.

When she got home for the second time, she saw the message light on the machine. It was from Todd; he had a meeting but he would be right home afterwards.

Fiona spent the rest of the day in a wonderful mood as she cleaned the house and prepared for what she hoped to be a very romantic evening. She wrote a note and taped it to the front door. It read: "Todd, what's happened to us? We used to be so close and now we are almost strangers. I miss you very much. I want to talk to you about us and I want to make us better, do you? Let's not talk right now though, let's play a little. Come on in and take your clothes off... I'll meet you in the bathtub."

When Todd got home, he read the note and suddenly felt this need to hug his wife and tell her how much he missed her. Inside the front door, he took off his clothes, noticed a vase of flowers on the table and took out a long-stemmed red rose. He went upstairs and noticed candles lit everywhere. It was beautiful and he couldn't believe she had done this for him. Todd walked into the bathroom and, like a vision, his wife was lying in the tub, bubbles all over her body. Her hair was pulled up with just a few strands hanging down and she looked lovely, more beautiful than he had ever seen her.

Todd slowly climbed into the tub as she handed him cold champagne that she had poured into their crystal wedding goblets.

The two stared at each other for what seemed like days. Todd took her glass from her hand, placed it, along with his, onto the floor and embraced her. Then they kissed passionately. They spent the rest of the evening loving each other, making love to one another, and getting back all those lost years and lost kisses.

When Fiona awoke the next morning, Todd had already left for work. She felt sad and wondered if in fact a difference had been made in their relationship. She got up, took a shower and went downstairs.

On the counter she noticed one of their framed wedding pictures, a note taped to it.

It read: "Fiona, my lovely, lovely wife. You are every breath I take and everything that makes me happy. I am a fool for being so distant and I can't explain it. I have been selfish and unkind and I was wrong. You are my love and you are my life, and I will never let you go that far away from me again. Thank you for a wonderful evening and for reminding me again how special you are and how lucky I am. I love you. Love Todd."

What a wonderful surprise! Fiona felt good inside. All her emptiness and loneliness dissolved. They were going to be okay and their marriage was good again.

She had to tell Angela, so she quickly got dressed and rushed to the park in hopes of seeing her there again. But Angela didn't come that day. In fact it was many months before Fiona saw her again, only it wasn't her, it was a picture in a book of angels.

Angela was Fiona's angel and she had come into Fiona's life to guide her in the direction that helped save their marriage. Every week now, Fiona went to the park and sat on the bench, but she never again went alone. Todd came with her. Now they were one of the beautiful couples sneaking kisses and secretly being watched by someone else who longed for the romance that they had once again found.

His Scent

The flight went well. Luckily I didn't have to sit next to, or listen to, any screaming kids.

What I was about to do was hard enough on my nerves; I didn't need anything else. The limo was going to pick me up and take me to his hotel room.

Why was I doing this? I knew he was married, but I just couldn't resist. I loved the way he made me feel and I was curious what a whole night alone with him would be like.

The limo picked me up and drove me to the hotel. After I checked in, I was taken to his room, the penthouse suite, of course. It was beautiful and I felt luxurious and spoiled. I was also just a little afraid of what lay ahead. He was out at a conference and wouldn't be back until three o'clock, so I had a few hours to pamper myself and prepare for what I hoped to be an exciting evening.

When he finally walked through the door, I felt myself begin to shake. I was afraid of what was going to happen and unsure of what I was supposed to do next. He came up to me and hugged me, calming and reassuring me, and warming me up with those amazing arms and shoulders. His hugs are spectacular. When he touches me I feel this need to let my fingers touch every inch of his body.

There was no hesitation; we went straight to bed. I felt good in his arms and warmed by his body as it touched mine. He kissed me and touched my body, making me shiver. He went down to his favorite place, between my legs, and licked me until I was wet and excited and desperately wanted him inside me. He loves it down there; I can sense how much he enjoys it and how happy it makes him to continue to taste me.

I was going crazy inside. I could hardly control myself as I grabbed hold of the pillows for support and scratched at the headboard with my recently manicured nails. He finally came up and nuzzled up to me. When he kissed me, I tasted myself. It was exciting. I wanted him and I wanted him bad. He slowly entered me and I could feel my breath shudder, he felt so good inside me. He moved in and out of me until we came together with a wetness only good sex could create.

Afterwards, we laid there, and I watched him as his breathing went from hard and fast to soft and controlled. I wrapped his arm around me. I loved being there with him and was pleased with my decision to make the trip.

We napped a short while, and then drank some wine. The wine was soft on my lips and tasted so good and went down easily, I was thirsty for more ...and hungry for him. We talked for a while, shared kisses, and then went back to bed. I couldn't tell if I was drunk from the wine or from the way he made me feel. The time we shared always blended into one magical moment.

The next morning, when we woke up, he said had to leave. It was weird. I felt as though I had just woken up from a wonderful dream and the whole evening before became suddenly unreal. I didn't want him to go. I watched him as he dressed and got himself ready for the conference. I wanted to tell him what a wonderful evening last night was, how much I enjoyed his company, and how thankful I was that he had set aside time just for me. But I couldn't get up the nerve, so I just sat there and watched him. I wanted to cry but I didn't want him to see it, so I held it in. He kissed me goodbye... and then he left.

I sat on the bed for a while. I stared at the crumpled sheets around me. I looked around the room, then focused on the bed we had made love in. I took a breath and inhaled his scent, which floated around me, and it warmed me up. It was then I realized; that should I never see him again, I still had that moment. It had been amazingly wonderful. In that short period of time, I felt incredibly loved.

And I never did see him again. I'm really not sure what happened to him or where he went or what he is doing. Sometimes the wind blows past me and I get a whiff of a familiar scent and I look around. If I close my eyes tight enough, he is there. I feel him near me, but he's nowhere in sight. My body moistens, my heart beats and I feel dampness between my legs. It's amazing how one man can have such an effect on you.

This happened years ago... yet I feel as though I just left his room.

My Darling Carina

It had been two long years since Carina had last made love. She had her son, Cody, to remind her of that. How could she ever forget? Just the memory of that time in her life would bring a smile to her face. It was an event that started out so strange, yet ended up so personal.

It began late at night after she and Eddie had yet another knockdown drag-out fight, which ended with her fleeing the apartment building. In her haste she bumped right into a man outside on the pavement as he was walking by. He was an older man, maybe in his middle forties, and very tall. He was also dressed all in black, which prompted her to think his attire matched her mood. He immediately became concerned at her tears and asked Carina if there was anything he could do or if she needed someone to talk to.

Against habit she agreed to talk with him. Besides, it was raining and she was too upset to argue. The two walked across the street to the coffee shop. She found Jasper; *that was his name*, to be a nice man, someone who didn't have to reach to find the right things to say. She felt she could trust him, so she told him everything about her relationship with Eddie. They talked for three hours. At the end of their conversation, Jasper offered her a room at his place until she figured out what it was she wanted to do. She agreed.

Jasper's place surprised her by its beauty and warmth. It was a two-story, three-bedroom apartment furnished like an old-fashioned Bed and Breakfast. Once inside the front door Carina felt invited, comfortable, and safe. After she got settled in, Jasper brought her a steaming cup of herb tea and a warm blanket. As she sipped it, Jasper suggested what she really needed was good night's sleep and then a lot of quiet time to sort herself out and figure out what exactly she needed.

After the fourth day, Jasper asked her to move in permanently. There was plenty of room, he said, and he could use the company. There was no pressure, he added. For her part, Carina knew she had to make plans, so a few days later she agreed to move in. That same day she returned to her old apartment to fetch her things and leave a note for Eddie. The note was simple. She told Eddie she didn't want anymore of his abuse and had decided to move on with her life. After that day, she never contacted him again.

Jasper was so good to Carina and spoiled her rotten. Their relationship eventually went beyond deep friendship; they needed one another. For her two-month "on-her-own" anniversary, Jasper took her out shopping and bought her a new wardrobe. Carina felt like a princess the way he pampered her and bought her presents. But it was far more than that. He respected her and listened to her when she talked. He made her feel special and important, she mattered to him.

Nevertheless, after five or six months, Carina decided to get a job and finally move out and find a place of her own. She realized that Jasper couldn't continue supporting her. Although financially he could afford it, she didn't feel right about not paying her fair share.

She did help around the house, however, doing the shopping, and she even cooked once in awhile. But it wasn't enough in her eyes. She wanted to offer more. When she finally told Jasper of her plans, and that she had found a job and planned to move out soon, he was terribly hurt and told her he didn't want her to leave. He said, of course, he was happy for her and proud that she had a job and prospects. But he explained that he had grown to care about her and enjoyed her company. He didn't want her to leave and begged her to stay. At the end of their talk, after a long silence, Carina agreed to stay, which made Jasper incredibly happy. To cement to deal, they decided to go out the next evening and celebrate.

The next day, Carina came home to find a gift-wrapped box on her bed. When she opened it, she found a stunning evening gown. With the gift was a note from Jasper, telling her he wanted her to feel like a princess that evening, and she would in that dress.

They both dressed up that night. Jasper had arranged for a limo to pick them up. Carina had never been treated this way. She felt so lucky to have found him, and for the first time in what seemed like forever, she was happy. They had a wonderful dinner with several bottles of champagne. Carina was drunk and happy and when she wrapped her arms around Jasper to thank him, she found herself kissing him. It was a soft, warm and loving kiss, and with it Carina felt something new, something she had never felt. When they pulled apart, Jasper looked at her and asked if she would spend the evening in his bed. She said, "yes."

They made love for the first time that night, and it continued throughout the rest of the weekend. They left the bed only for meals. They discovered each other's bodies; they talked about everything, and they fell asleep in each other's arms. Originally, Carina hadn't been attracted to Jasper, but as she got to know him and as they made love, she realized that she had fallen in love with him.

When she woke up Monday morning Jasper was gone. There was a note on the dining room table. The note read:

> "*My darling Carina. I have longed to touch your body and you gave it to me with little hesitation. You have made a lonely man very happy. Please forgive me for taking advantage of you that way, but my body was filled with this need to have you and to be a part of you. I enjoyed this weekend very much, and hope you enjoyed it, too.*
>
> *Love Jasper*"

She read the note again and smiled. This was the first time anyone had ever really loved her and although she had had many loves in her life, she had never felt the way she did about Jasper towards any of them.

In the days to follow, Jasper and Carina made love every evening and Carina moved into his bedroom. Jasper taught her the fine art of making love, pleasing her in ways she didn't know were possible. Ever gentle and sweet and considerate, he never did anything she didn't want and centered his every attention on her needs and happiness. For her part, during their first year together, Carina refined her ways of pleasing him, which brought both unforgettable passion. It became her pleasure to find new ways to please him.

One morning, Carina decided to surprise Jasper with breakfast in bed. Just eggs wouldn't do, she thought, as she prepared French toast with fresh berries and whipped cream. It was a wonderful breakfast and Jasper loved it. He hugged her tightly, kissed her and said, "*Carina, I love you, you make me very happy.*"

She saw a tear rolling down his cheek, but looked away pretending she hadn't seen. In the weeks to follow, their relationship grew stronger. Unfortunately, it never really went anywhere. Carina enjoyed their time together, but soon found herself yearning for something more. She never talked about marriage or that she wanted to give him children.

As the weeks turned into months, Carina noticed Jasper change. He didn't seem quite himself anymore. He always looked haggard, ate little, even when she tempted him with her specialty dishes. And they hardly made love anymore. He would only ask her to sit next to him and hold his hands, and sometimes read poetry to him.

Carina finally admitted to herself that Jasper was ill. It happened so fast; she reflected. Within the month, Jasper was bedridden, diagnosed with brain cancer. His prognosis was two months left to live. Carina became his dedicated caregiver.

Jasper never mentioned family, so Carina was in this alone. As for his financial affairs, Jasper met with his lawyers and advisers, but never involved Carina in these meetings. She did whatever he wanted and didn't ask any questions.

One morning, while she was downstairs fixing his breakfast, she heard a thump in the upstairs bedroom. Jasper, she thought frantically, and rushed upstairs only to find him sprawled on the floor by his bed. Dead. Tenderly, with great strength, Carina lifted her lover's body from the floor, her eyes full of tears, and struggled to lay him out on his bed. Heaving with the effort and crying, she noticed a document in his hands. It looked to be the beginning of a letter to her. The letter read:

> *"My Dear Sweet Carina. You have been so good to me and showed me what true love is. I want you to know I have taken care of you, but never will it come close to how well you have cared for me, and in no way will it ever repay you for the kindness and warmth you've showed me. You fill my heart with love. Carina, I love you and I hope you..."*

The letter ended abruptly.

He was writing it when he died, she thought, but she didn't have to read it in its entirety. She understood what he was trying to say and she loved him too, very much.

The funeral was quiet, with only the lawyers and her in attendance. Afterwards, it was hard to go back to the apartment knowing he wouldn't be there and she would never see him again. A few days passed and she hadn't even gotten off the couch. When the phone rang, it startled her. It was one of the lawyers requesting a meeting with her.

After the meeting, Carina went back to the old coffee shop where she and Jasper first met. She reread his last letter as she absorbed the information the lawyers had just given her. Jasper had arranged to sell his apartment, donating most of the proceeds to the homeless shelters around the city. For Carina he had left the remainder of his assets, totaling 3.4 million dollars.

Carina went back to the apartment, packed her belongings, took an old photo of Jasper and left. Four days later she found out she was three months pregnant. She smiled as she read his obituary, clipped from yesterday's paper, which said he didn't have any living relatives.

The obituary was mistaken. He did; he just wouldn't ever know about it.

Fantasies and Flat Tires

Kaitlyn loved married life and having a family, but deep down inside she felt a part of her was missing, that perhaps she needed some other type of physical satisfaction.

When she and Jason first met, their sex life was wild and full of passion. She wanted him at all times and together he fulfilled her every imaginable sexual desire. But after marriage and the first child came along, the chemistry began to fizzle until eventually it slowed down to almost nothing. Kaitlyn herself wanted sex as much as always – in fact, she would have had it a few times a day if her husband was willing – but Jason wasn't willing. It seemed he had lost his once rampant sexual desire for her.

Kaitlyn's eyes and fantasies went elsewhere. Even driving down the highway these days, she would notice men, get their attention, and send them a smile. More recently, she summoned the nerve to pull her breast from her blouse and fondle it as two men in a Mustang convertible watched her eagerly. The idea of arousing strangers soon excited her and made her feel wanted. She would often fantasize about meeting up with a mysterious, good-looking man and having exhausting sex with him.

One day on the freeway, she noticed a stunning man driving a Ford truck. He smiled and waved at her, she smiled and waved back, and this went on for a few miles. All of a sudden she heard a loud noise and her car swerved across the road. She realized she'd had a blowout. She quickly pulled off, got out, headed for the trunk, and then stopped in her tracks when she realized she didn't know how to change the spare. She was stranded. Kaitlyn called her husband on the cell phone. He was on his way, he told her, but she was going to have to wait.

By this time, however, the young man in the Ford truck, pulled up behind her and offered her a lift. He told her he had pulled off the freeway and circled back to help her. Kaitlyn got in, feeling nervous and excited sitting in the truck next to him, not knowing what would happen next, but anxiously awaiting the outcome. He took an exit off the freeway that turned into a private road. Up ahead she noticed an old deserted barn. He seemed to notice it as well and headed toward it and pulled up in front.

After he parked the truck, he looked at her and said: "You and I have something we need to take care of and if we don't do it quickly I think I am going to burst and I don't think either of us wants that."

Kaitlyn watched him take off his shirt, her eyes becoming dreamy at the tanned mounds of muscle of his arms and shoulders. He opened his door, stepped out, came around to her door and helped her out of the truck. When she stepped down onto the ground, she had to look up at him; he was so tall and so huge. In her nervousness her skin perspired and her body tingled from head to toe.

He picked her up, carried her to the barn and placed her down on to the piles of hay strewn all over the floor.

He started to unbuckle his belt, then looked down at her and said,

"Before I go any further, I need to know that you want this as much as I think you do. I won't continue unless you show me how much you want it."

Kaitlyn stood up and showed him. She slowly took off one item of clothing at a time until she was naked. She then helped him undress. As she did she kissed his chest and touched his arms, shoulders, chest, and stomach. Taking a deep breath, she then moved down towards his penis where she hesitated for a minute before she touched it.

Aching with desire, she took him with her to the floor and they started kissing. He kissed her neck, her breasts, her stomach, before Kaitlyn felt his hot breath moistening the space between her legs. With a roughness she had so often imagined, he entered her, grabbing her ass for support. She wanted to touch him, but her body was petrified with ecstasy. In an instant his body began to jackhammer inside her, bringing her to heights of passion she never thought she'd ever experience again. Together they orgasmed, unbelievably, and he collapsed on top of her, both dripping in sweat.

Some time later she felt his tongue licking her left nipple and his fingers on her right one, a new experience for Kaitlyn. Her body started to spasm uncontrollably. Suddenly, she became a different woman, someone in some book somewhere. She aggressively reached down between his legs, grabbed his incredibly hard penis, and moved her mouth down around it. She loved the way his body shivered with excitement, her newfound power.

Kaitlyn continued to move her mouth up and down very quickly on his penis, then slow her pace to tease him and make him beg. She licked and sucked on him as if on a delicious ice cream ice cream, until she felt the creamy white splash of his excitement squirt into her mouth. How long has it been, Kaitlyn? She silently asked herself. Giddy and excited, like a kid in a soda shop, she wanted more.

He reached down for her and brought her up towards him, saying, "It's my turn, let me do the same for you."

He leaned over to his jeans, reached in the pocket and pulled out a blue bandanna. This he tied around her wrists and then tied her to a post. Putting her legs over his shoulders, he started licking between her legs. Once there, he quickly located a spot with his tongue she didn't know existed. Every time his tongue touched it, her body went into spasms. Each time she squirmed, the bandanna became tighter and although it hurt, it made her even more excited and she screamed out: "Now... I want you now!"

Laughing, he grabbed a hold of his penis and said, "You want this, sweetheart? Okay, here it is."

And he entered her and began his stroke. While he moved in and out of her, he untied the bandanna and tenderly kissed her reddened and sore wrists. Then, as he came, he kissed her nipples, her neck and then gently rested his lips on hers until he had reached his climax and dropped down on top of her.

As they dressed, she asked him to take her to the nearest gas station so she could call someone to help her. Then they walked back to the truck and headed down the road. Driving along, she heard Billy Ray Cyrus's song "Achy, Breaky Heart" playing on the radio.

All she could think of was her achy, breaky body as she drifted off to sleep.

Suddenly she heard someone saying: "Kaitlyn, Kaitlyn wake up."

Thinking it was the young man wanting more, she woke right up. Instead, she was startled to see her husband standing by her car with a tow truck driver.

Kaitlyn couldn't quite believe it was a dream; it had seemed so real.

When they got home that evening, her husband handed her a blue bandanna and said, "Here Sweetie, I found this in the back seat. You or one of the kids must have left it in the car." and he handed it to her.

Staring at it, she wondered. Had it happened, she asked herself. No matter, she shrugged. She had a spark in her eyes, some romance in her life, and she had the sexual desire she had lost so long ago.

Pure Pleasure

I was supposed to meet Niki for dinner, but when I arrived at the restaurant, Niki wasn't there yet, so I sat at the bar and ordered a drink. The friendly bartender did his best to keep me entertained while I waited for my friend. I ordered an appetizer and another drink.

After about an hour, still no Niki. The bartender, Tom, asked me if I wanted a shot of tequila. I told him I wasn't a big tequila fan, but he assured me this stuff would soon change my opinion. He was right; it was good. When I remarked how good it was, Tom told me it was called *Patron*, a more expensive tequila than the *Cuervo Gold* which I disliked. It made the hair on my arms stand up and my whole body got warm. He confided to me that *Patron* made him horny. I laughed. But as the evening went on, and the Patron was poured, I began wondering what Tom would look like without his clothes on.

As the minutes passed, my head lightened and my senses keened, the music from the live band insinuated itself. An old Fleetwood Mac tune caused me to sway in my chair to the music. By then I hadn't the slightest idea what time it was, nor did I care. After three tequila shots later I felt just fine and even better about Niki's no-show.

Tom leaned over the bar toward my stool and took my hands in his. Leaning further, he stared into my eyes, smiled seductively, and caressed my hands. He asked me if I wanted to dance. I felt self-conscious about my quickly moistening hands, wondering if he noticed my hands were sweating, as had my whole body as soon as he touched me.

I said yes, of course, I'd love to dance.

Tom led me onto the dance floor. Although there was music, laughter, and the normal bar noises, we might as well have been alone. The music moved around our bodies, bringing us closer together. I could feel him harden as he pressed close to me. He rubbed his lips against my neck and bit me.

Briefly startled, his bite sent shivers through me. It was incredibly sexy. He softly licked the spot where he had bit me, then kissed it. He took his finger from where it rested at my lower back, and slowly trailed it up along my spine and traced it around my neckline. I felt a little like one of Dracula's victims as he concentrated on my neck, touching, biting, kissing as if I were his prospective dinner... or desert.

The music had ended long since. How long ago the song stopped I wasn't sure, but we continued circling each other, staring into each other's eyes, neither able to let go.

Finally, he took my hand and walked me back to my seat at the bar; he had to get back to work. By then I was oblivious as to where I was or whom I was with. But reality returned as I sat back down at my stool and watched Tom make drinks.

Dizzy suddenly, I went down the hall to the ladies' room where I splashed cold water on my face. I felt much better. As I walked out of the door, Tom was coming out of the men's room and we bumped into one another.

We looked at each other, frozen, until he grabbed me by the shoulders and pushed me up against the wall. He asked me if I wanted him. I managed a yes; I couldn't say much else. It was a struggle just to get this one word out.

Tom kissed me hard, the pressure of his soft lips intense, powerful. He held me against the wall and we continued kissing. Someone walked by, but we didn't care. Finally, Tom pulled away and looked me straight in the eyes. There was no beating around the bush with him, I knew. He asked me straight out if I would stay until closing and be with him that evening. Again, I said, "Yes."

Before I knew it, it was last call. The music was over and people were reluctantly filtering out. The employees were busy cleaning up while Tom put everything away behind the bar. Meanwhile, I tried to calculate how many shots of tequila I had drunk that evening. I couldn't, but I was definitely feeling the effects. I kept watching Tom as he worked and all I could think of was his skin touching mine. He'd look over at me once in a while and give me that smile. Boy, was he smooth... but I loved it.

Finally at 2:30 A.M., there was only the two of us. Tom locked the door, walked over to me and took my hand. We walked up the stairs and around the corner on the second floor and went to the liquor storeroom. It was small and smelled of stale liquor and cardboard.

Tom turned off the light, leaving the stone silent room pitch black. All I could hear was his breathing and my heart beating. I saw nothing, but felt everything.

I reached out for him, grabbed his shoulders and squeezed them hard. Then I took his shirt off and unbuckled his belt. I quickly unzipped his pants pulled them down and took them off. I got down on my knees and pulled off his boxers, slightly scratching him with my nails. I grabbed a hold of his now throbbing dick and put it in my mouth, kissing and sucking on it, nibbling at it ever so slightly. I could hear his palm slap the nearest wall as if to prop himself against it.

He was breathing hard and he made gurgling sounds of pleasure. Finally, I felt him tense up and come in my mouth like an exploding volcano. He tasted so good and I was hungry for more. I stood up and wiped his cum off my face with the back of my hand, and then we eagerly kissed.

Tom turned me around so I faced up against the wall. He entered me from behind and pushed up against me. He increased his thrusts, going faster and faster, until we both screamed. All I could think was… Oh my God, this man is amazing.

When he came, he wrapped his arms around me. Placing his hands on my breasts, he pinched my nipples hard; so hard I flinched in pain. It hurt so good. We stood there in the dark, our bodies wet with sweat, neither of us moving.

He pulled away, turned me around to face him, and kissed me.

Then he asked me my name. All this time he never even knew my name. I borrowed a line from the *Pretty Woman* movie and asked him what he wanted it to be.

"Pure Pleasure," he replied.

All I could do was smile.

We got dressed and went back downstairs. Tom finished locking up the bar and walked me to my car. He gave me a nice hug and told me I was a good dancer. I thanked him for teaching me the fine art of good tequila and then I got in my car. I started the car, lit a cigarette and drove home.

The clock on the radio said it was 4:37 a.m. We had been up in that little room for over two hours. When I got home, I threw my clothes in the hamper and jumped in the shower. The water felt good as it splashed all over my naked body. I looked down at my chest. There I found my breasts pocked with multiple little bruises. He really did bite hard, I thought. I laughed, then smiled and I thanked God I walked into that bar last night.

And I went to bed happy.

Red Checkered Flannel

It was one of those days; one of those times when I wished Calgon could *really* take me away. I knew that wasn't going to happen, so I continued packing the kids' lunches and hurried them off to school. Home again, as I sat in the sudden silence I thought of my life. I had been married to Craig for fifteen years, I reflected, and though most of those years were reasonably happy, the marriage was now only one of convenience, one lacking in love and affection.

Was it too much to ask to be touched once in a while?

These thoughts never left me.

One day after dropping off the kids, I decided to go for a drive. I wasn't sure where I was going or what I was going to do when I got there, but I knew I needed something to spice up my life a little. And I decided to find it. The weather hinted towards rain, yet not following through, but still dark, drizzly and quiet. I let the road take me where it wanted me to go. I was wearing an old T-shirt, blue jeans, and a pair of Keds. I looked in my rearview and noticed my hair was falling loosely around my face. No matter, I thought, I certainly wasn't going anywhere that required a dress code. I turned on the radio and sang along with Reba on the C&W station.

In minutes my spirits lifted, I smiled mischievously, feeling like a good girl on a bad mission.

After an hour or so, I came across and old saloon-style bar &

grill. Out in front were parked over a dozen Harleys side-by-side in formation, along with some beat-up trucks. I parked my fire red BMW right in there with them. It looked out of place. Was I, I asked myself.

As I entered the bar and looked around, my Keds stuck to the wood floors covered with sawdust and dirt and cigarette wrappers sprinkled about. I noticed a pool table in the corner and a few tables scattered carelessly around the room.

I hesitated briefly, letting my eyes adjust, then headed towards the bar. On my way I felt several pairs of eyes watching me. At the bar I asked the bartender for a glass of Chardonnay. He nodded and returned with a Budweiser and a shot of Jack Daniels. I paid him and said thanks.

I held up the Bud and the shot with either hand, shrugged at their foreign nature, then partook. I liked it. So much, in fact, I had three more.

After the third one I started feeling funny, kind of feather light but iron tough. I felt like I could do anything or be anyone and no one would be the wiser. For the first time in a long while I wasn't a wife, a mother, a maid, a cook or anything else. I was just me, and I really liked the feeling.

While nursing my fourth whiskey and wash, I suddenly felt a warm breath on my neck. I turned, looked, then my eyes shot up to the most ruggedly handsome man I had ever seen. He had huge broad shoulders and blinding blue eyes and wore Levis like no man I had ever seen. In a husky voice he asked me if I wanted to dance, but before I could answer, he took my hand and led me onto to the dance floor.

We danced for a while to old songs I hadn't heard in years. I felt comfortable in his arms, safe and warm, and so far away from everything that mattered. Before I knew it, I was perched on the back of his bike as we sped down a winding road, the wind whipping my face. Minutes later, he turned onto a dirt road at the end of which I saw an old rustic cabin, which I figured was his place.

I wasn't nervous or scared; but strangely perfectly at ease with everything that was happening. I knew I needed this, that I wanted it, and I was damn well going to enjoy it.

He helped me off the bike, looked into my eyes and asked me if this was something I really wanted to do. I nodded yes, to which he picked me up and carried me into the cabin and placed me gently on his bed.

I watched as he took off his jeans, his red-checkered flannel shirt and the whitest pair of boxers I had ever seen. As he stood there naked, I stared, stunned with his handsome features, firm muscles, and his huge penis. He came over to me, and took off my T-shirt, Keds and jeans. I sat on the bed only in my lavender lace bra and panties, feeling just a little out of place, and waited for him to make the next move.

He did, touching me everywhere, slowly, and so knowingly – as though he and I were old lovers. Then he lay me down on my back. With his teeth he pulled off my panties as his whiskers tickled my legs. He brought his mouth back up between my legs and licked me.

It felt so good.

He climbed up on top of the bed and lay his body gently atop mine. He entered me with a power that left me numb. We made love for what seemed like hours in positions I've never even read about. When we finished, he picked me up and carried me to the shower, where he lathered my body and rinsed me off.

Afterwards, when I reached for my shirt, it ripped as I pulled it out from under the bed, so he handed me his red-checkered flannel shirt. It was soft and smelled like him; I loved wearing it. We finished dressing, got back on the bike and rode back to the bar where we had met.

When I got off the motorcycle, I hoped we might have a drink and perhaps exchange names. Instead, as I started to speak, he silenced me. He wrapped his hand around my neck, pulled me close to him, kissed me hard, and said goodbye as he turned around and walked back into the bar.

That was it; he was gone. I really didn't know what I was supposed to do next until I looked at my watch and realized I had forty-five minutes until I had to pick Alexis and Stevie up at school, so I jumped in the car and left.

That night I couldn't get my handsome mystery man out of my head. After feeding, bathing and putting the kids to bed, I called my husband Craig up to our bedroom. When he walked in, all I had on was the red-checkered flannel shirt tied at the waist, some red thong underwear and a pair of old red cowboy boots I had left over from a Halloween costume one year. At first, he stared at me with a surprised look, but soon the growing bulge in his pajama pants caught his attention. And mine.

I climbed up on the bed and motioned for him to join me. Then I attacked him with the passion of a wildcat; we became two ravenous animals grabbing at each. It had been such a long time since we had done this; I think we were both a little surprised.

Craig never asked what had come over me that evening. And I've never mentioned it to anyone, except for now, what happened that day. But I will say that every time I see a man on a Harley, I go put that shirt on and look for my husband!

The Kiss

Troy has the most amazing smile; it brightens the room for me. And those eyelashes, the way they tickle my face when he kisses me.

When I first saw him I couldn't resist. It was too hard. And he's a good man, too, with an incredible heart. It was lucky really, my meeting him when I did, since it occurred quite by accident. Rather mundane: he came to our office to repair a typewriter of all things. I was the only one in the office that day.

Since it was a slow day, we talked – about family and friends and things that keep us busy. Meanwhile I watched him while he worked. I couldn't help noticing his nice shoulders, firm arms, and those hands of his, beautiful and rugged all at once, an artisan's hands with signs of hard work in every line and tendon. I wanted to touch him; I wanted him to touch me. As I watched him work, I fantasized about what it would be like to kiss him. As he worked I closed my eyes a few times and pictured his soft, full lips pressed against mine. It was hard to concentrate on my work with him so close by in the room.

After a while, he came into my office. He told me he had to go back to their warehouse to pick up a few parts and would return shortly. I watched him walk out the door to his truck, and felt my body ache for him.

When he returned an hour later, he silently walked up to my desk and placed a rose in front of me. I looked up and asked him what it was for, and he told me it was *a beautiful flower for a beautiful woman*. I just smiled. He was so handsome and so sweet, and in such a short time was driving me wild.

Then he took a hold of my hand and caressed it with his fingers, and worked his hands up to tenderly massage my arms, meanwhile complimenting my soft skin. He brought my fingers to his lips and kissed them, all the while his eyes fixed on mine; kissing one finger... another... then another. He kissed my hand, moved up my arm to my shoulder, biting it; not too hard but it affected me deeply. Then he kissed my neck, my chin, my cheeks, my eyes and finally my lips. His kisses were soft and warm, he was such a passionate kisser; he made me tingle everywhere. Leaving me excited, he suddenly let go of me and walked over to the door, locked it and then closed the blinds.

I was nervous, and my heart was beating so fast I was afraid he could hear it. I didn't know what to say... but I knew I wanted him to touch me.

I watched him slowly walk back toward me, his eyes still pinned to mine. He pulled me close to him and took me into his arms. He felt so strong. While the radio softly played a slow song in the background, he helped me up and took me around the waist. We started dancing slowly to the music and he held me tightly as we moved together. He looked down at me and very slowly brought his lips to mine, holding them there for just a few seconds. Then, parting them with his tongue he kissed me. The kiss lasted an eternity, sending chills down my spine, raising the hairs on my arms and leaving goose bumps all over my body. His lips were strong, yet the pressure was so soft. He licked my lips and closed his eyes as he tasted me.

He took my hand, walked me over to the couch in the lobby and pulled me down next to him. He skillfully took off my shirt, slowly unbuttoning one button at a time, never taking his eyes off me. He unhooked my bra and took it off, and his hands brushed gently over my breasts. His soft hands felt like velvet against my skin. As he touched me, I could feel my nipples harden with excitement and the moistness grow between my legs.

He leaned over and kissed my breasts, licking my nipples and fondling the soft flesh with his fingers. Each of his hands found and cupped a breast as he kissed me again, slowly and passionately. I flushed, my body temperature rising, the wetness between my legs pulsing. I eagerly awaited him to make love to me.

We explored each other's bodies, kissing and touching and pleasing until finally neither of us could wait any longer and we made love. He entered me slowly and carefully, showing me a tenderness I've never felt. He ran his fingers through my hair, lightly pushing it away from my face as he kissed me. I felt the hot beads of sweat drop from his forehead onto my chest, tickling me as they cooled and beaded down and across my breast. I was mesmerized with his face, his close-eyed concentration as he moved confidently in and out of me until he stopped briefly and abruptly, then arch backwards and shout in total euphoria.

We lay together on the couch, our bodies wet with sweat. I

smiled as I felt his heart beating rapidly against my chest. While we lay there, we talked about the beauty of what we had just shared. I felt compelled to tell him I was married. I tried to explain my longtime unhappiness, but saw my words disturbed him.

Still I persisted. I tried to explain to him about my ten-year marriage to a man who paid more attention to the television than to me, and whose sex life rarely included me. And about the two children who made a quick exit impossible, (though my husband had broken up the family a long time ago). But I was too afraid to do anything about it.

We silently got up and put our clothes back on, a vague but obvious uneasiness in the air. By now he couldn't look at me at all.

Troy, that was his name, left his business card with me after he finished the repairs, and asked me to call him if I ever figured out what I was going to do with my life. It broke my heart to see him go, and when he walked out that door, I knew right then what I needed to do.

I went home that evening, packed a suitcase for myself and for the kids, and moved out. I started the divorce proceedings the next day. It took a few months before my husband agreed to anything, but we finally managed to get the papers signed. Within six months we were legally divorced. I decided I wouldn't call Troy until I was settled into my own place and had some time to think about what I needed and what was best for me.

Finally, months later, I sat down at the table and pulled out his business card, now tattered and torn and barely readable. I picked up the phone and called. The receptionist answered and I gave her my name. I stayed on hold for what seemed like hours, forced to listen to elevator music, while my heart was racing out of control and beads of sweat built on my forehead.

Suddenly, there he was, his voice summoning up such wonderful memories. We spent the first five minutes on small talk, but I couldn't stand the tension any longer.

I blurted out, "I'm divorced and I miss you so much."

We cried and we laughed and planned to meet the following day.

Our meeting went perfect. I knew right then that I had met the man of my dreams, my partner and my soul mate.

We've been married now for ten years and I've never been happier. I wish we had met under better circumstances, but I believe things happen for a reason. It was the kiss I remember most, the way his lips gently touched mine and we've been kissing ever since.

Rekindled Passions

As she pulled into the driveway, Kelly tightly closed her eyes, eyes as blue as the ocean sweeping before her, and prayed this weekend would prove to be everything she wished for.

She had coaxed Daniel into coming on the 'work weekend' premise: he could work on his reports while she shot some photographs for the magazine. Ironically fitting, she thought, since their marriage was more a business partnership these days, any lovemaking now only a dim fond memory of their early days. This trip to the famed Passions Cove was her last ditch attempt to bring passion and love back into their lives.

She walked towards the door, juggling her props and glancing at her watch. Daniel would be along in an hour. As she hesitated in the entryway she looked towards the French doors and saw they opened up to a lavish garden and a view of the ocean beyond. It all screamed of romance, she thought before proceeding in. Kelly placed the $110.00 bottle of champagne in the crystal bucket that stood on the counter of the kitchenette. Then she walked to the sound system and put on one of her sexy CD's. She found appropriate spots for the gorgeous teal candles that she brought, and lit them. With a hopeful smile, she went upstairs and put her bag on the bed. She opened it and gently lifted the delicate white lacy bustier from her bag and laid it on the bed, before unpacking the rest of the outfit she hoped would seduce him away from his books and numbers. She quickly dressed for his arrival.

Forty-five minutes later, Kelly heard Daniel's car pull-up and she quickly ran down the stairs to lay down on the carpet, next to the fire. He rang the doorbell. He rang it again. When he tried the doorknob the door was ajar. He walked in.

"Kelly? Are you in here?" She didn't answer. "Wow, this place is really nice," he remarked. "Honey? Kelly? Are you here?"

She heard his steps approach and stop. He must be taking it all in, Kelly smiled to herself – the incredible view... the champagne...

And finally Kelly, half-naked, lying before the fire.

Daniel stood stunned. Through her half-shut eyes she saw passion and love fill his.

The feelings written on his face showed his surprise as if he was trying to remember how very long it had been since they had made love or shared any kind of intimacy.

Daniel dropped his briefcase to the floor, threw his coat onto the back of the couch and slowly walked over to his beautiful wife. He went to his knees, leaned over and kissed her, looking intently into her eyes. He seemed to re-appreciate their ocean blueness, the same eyes that had caught his attention so many years before. He smiled at his incredibly beautiful wife. She saw the realization come to his businessman's brain: this wasn't going to be a work-related trip at all.

Kelly helped him off with his shirt, unbuttoning one button at time, slowly pulling it from his shoulders, gently caressing the softness of his bare arms, as she let the shirt fall to the floor. She kissed his chest and reached up to touch his face. It had been a long time... way too long. It was like their first time. The touch of his fingers against her skin, the kiss of her sweet lips on his chest, made them both shiver. Kelly helped Daniel take off his clothes, kissing every inch of his tanned, athletic body. He moaned and he smiled as they shared mutual feelings of pleasure as she found her way towards his penis, now throbbing and begging for her touch.

She played with it at first, letting her fingers caress each fold of the skin before she placed it in her mouth, letting her tongue linger over it's hardness. Her mouth swallowed it until she could feel it barely touching her throat. She moved her mouth up and down until he couldn't stand it any longer... until he couldn't control it... and he came... and she swallowed and smiled, knowing how much she had just pleased her husband. They continued to take turns pleasing one another, kissing and tenderly touching every inch of one another's bodies until finally they we were both completely spent with exhaustion and then they fell asleep.

When Kelly woke up, Daniel was curled up next to the fire, sound asleep and snoring. She loved him so much. This weekend was so important and Kelly would do whatever it took to make their marriage work.

She got up and went to the kitchen to get dinner ready. She had planned everything so well: the champagne was chilling, the crab was cracked and cleaned, and the salad was in the bowl.

As she sliced the bread, she heard Daniel stirring and she listened as he lazily padded in her direction. He came up behind her, kissed her neck and wrapped his big strong arms around her until she was breathless. She felt safe and loved... everything she had missed and had longed for.

They stood there for a long moment until Daniel broke the silence: "Kelly, I'm sorry for not paying more attention to our marriage. I love you so much and you mean everything to me. My heart aches at the thought of possibly losing you. Thank you for this, for everything ... for loving me and for giving me another chance."

She turned around to face him and they kissed.

Dinner was a success. After they finished off the champagne, they opened a cold bottle of Chardonnay. They took the wine, two glasses and a blanket out to the beach. As the sun slowly set, its orange and red flames sweeping across the water, they drank the wine and talked about forever.

With only the light from the neighboring houses and the quarter moon's dim light in the clear sky, they found themselves rolling around on the blanket like teenagers. They kissed and fondled one another, ripping off their clothes until finally they both lay there naked, their bare bodies melted together by the heat and sweat of their newfound passion.

Slowly, Daniel climbed on top of Kelly, looked into her eyes and he entered her. She closed her eyes as he went in further, feeling every inch of him. Her body quivered as he touched her. She arched up just enough to feel him go a little further and then they moved in rhythm with the ocean as the waves crashed up along the shore.

"Daniel..." Kelly whispered. "Daniel, Honey, this is wonderful. I missed this so much... I've missed you so much."

Daniel put his fingers against her lips. "Kelly... shhh... just hold me."

They lay there together staring at the sky, watching for falling stars and listening to the music of the ocean, drifting....

They were startled by a gruff voice: "Excuse me. You people shouldn't be here on this beach at this time of morning. Get yourselves a hotel... or go home."

Kelly and Daniel giggled as they watched the old man walk back down the beach, his grumbles slowly diminishing in the crash of surf.

They got dressed and went back to their romantic house on the beach to finish where they had left off ... making love.

The next morning Kelly woke up to breakfast in bed. They ate together and laughed and kissed.

"Hurry, get out of bed, sleepyhead," Daniel teased and took her hand. "I have another surprise for you."

She followed him into the bathroom. The tub was filled to overflowing with bubbles and dozens of scented candles were lit about the room. He helped her into the warm, bubbly water and then joined her.

She opened the shutters, only to find that all that lay outside of them was the ocean and the sunshine. As she sat there enjoying the moment, she noticed Daniel staring at her. "What are you looking at?"

"At you," he replied, "and I can't believe how beautiful you are.

Look at you. Your hair is tousled on top of your head, bubbles are surrounding your amazing body and your eyes are the same color as the ocean. I would be crazy not to grab you right this second and make mad passionate love to you."

And he did.

They spent the day walking along the beach, holding hands and collecting shells, talking about where they went wrong and what they could do differently. Then their eyes found an old couple, perhaps in their eighties, sitting on a giant piece of driftwood. They were holding hands, the woman leaning against the man, her head resting on his shoulder.

Daniel and Kelly watched spellbound for minutes in silence.

Then: "I want us to be that way. I want us to grow old together. I don't want us to lose the passion."

Kelly began to cry. As Daniel wiped away her tears, he comforted her: "Kelly, I want us to grow old together, too; to never let go of what we've found this weekend. I love you."

"I love you too Daniel."

As they packed their things and cleaned up the house, Kelly walked from room to room of this magical house, remembering each moment that had brought them back together. Daniel confessed to her that when she had first asked him to come there, he had been angry and felt it was a waste of time. He could have worked just as easy at their house or at the office. But, he added, when he first walked through the door and saw her lying there on the floor by the fire, he was confused. Then came relief – because all along he had known they were drifting apart and for whatever reason, he couldn't make the right moves to make things better.

Kelly closed her eyes as she had when she had first pulled in the driveway and sighed. The weekend had worked as she hoped. They locked the door behind them and walked to their cars holding hands. At their cars parked side-by-side, they hugged each other and couldn't let go for a long time.

They kissed passionately, until Daniel winked at her: "Race ya home."

Dancing In the Rain

Two young lovers are lying naked together on the beach, oblivious to the darkening sky and threatening rain. Eventually the rain pours down on them and soaks them completely.

After putting on their sopping clothing, they run up to their car only to find that the keys are locked inside. They frantically look around for any shelter and notice a house nearby. But it looks closed and abandoned.

As it proves to be when they get there. They try every door and window, but the place is secure. Desperate, they break a small window by the back door and enter the kitchen. They find the light switch doesn't work, nor the heater; the power is off. Inside the living room they find the furniture covered in sheets, looking as though the place hasn't been occupied in a long time.

The two find a candelabrum by the fireplace, and, using his cigarette lighter, the man carefully lights each candle. They build a fire in the fireplace and take their clothes off to dry in front of it. Then they cuddle up under a blanket the woman finds in a basket next to the side of the fire grate.

As the fire warms their naked bodies, they continue where they have left off before the rain interrupted them. They make love moving from the floor to the couch and then to the hearth of the fireplace.

When they are finished, they decide to explore the old house. Upstairs they find a trunk in one of the bedrooms filled with old clothing and decide to play dress-up.

He puts on an old double-breasted tuxedo and she puts on an old-fashioned ball gown. It is an eerie coincidence: everything fits perfectly. They admire one another and begin dancing around the room to music they mutually seem to hear.

Suddenly it is decades in the past. The house is alive with activity; the lights are on, music playing, people talking, glasses clinking, and smells of food emanating from the kitchen. An elegant party is in full swing, its complement of guests dressed in the finest silk and velvet.

Beautiful music plays; people dance.

A couple in the center of the room moves elegantly across the dance floor in perfect rhythm to the music.

The song finishes, and the young couple glide together, still dancing in the midst of the dust and cobwebs – illuminated only by the light of the fire guiding them their movements.

They wake up the next morning, more in love than ever before. The rain has stopped, so they board up the broken window and leave the house holding hands and smiling. They find a service station just minutes down the road and arrange to have their car opened.

As they drive away, they pass the abandoned house and notice a 'For Sale' sign in the weedy front yard. They look at one another, smile, and quickly write down the number of the realtor.

Paradise

The two-dozen red roses were delivered. The card read: "Saturday, 1:00 p.m., meet me at 3335 Birch Street #17 @ Passions Cove. Love, Wayne."

Heather read the card over and over. She had been dating Wayne on and off for three years now. Although she loved him, he was married and it was difficult loving a married man. He would make so many promises and make so many plans, too many of which he canceled. It was hard to take him seriously.

She picked up the phone and dialed.

"Hi Wayne, it's me Heather. Thank you for the flowers; you know how much I love roses. I'd love to meet you, but you know how I feel. I can't keep doing this. I can't give myself to you any longer, knowing full well that you will never be able give yourself to me. I can't go with you. I love you and I'll miss you. Bye."

Heather hung up after leaving the message on his voice mail at work and started crying. She loved him so much. There was nothing more she wanted than to spend a weekend away with him at some romantic getaway, but she knew it was finally time for her to stop seeing him.

Later that day, Heather heard a knock on her door. When she opened it, before her stood the most handsome man she had ever seen...had ever loved. Wayne. Silly, cute, lovable Wayne.

"Honey," he pleaded, "please come with me this weekend. I have made so many plans and I have a surprise for you. Please?"

Then he gave her that look. The one that rendered her defenseless, the one where he tilts his head slightly, and looks up, batting his long lashes and pouting like a small child.

It worked. They left.

It was a two-hour drive, but it was, as always, pleasant. He never let go of her hand. They kissed at every stoplight and he kept repeating how happy he was that she had come. He looked so yummy in his jeans and his whiter-than-white shirt. The Cheshire Cat, driving with his grin a mile wide. Why did she always give in, she asked herself. Why hadn't she said no this time and stuck to it? Why didn't she ever say no? She knew why. As they drove along the coast, Heather found herself getting excited. By the time they pulled into the driveway, Heather was dying to make love to Wayne.

From the outside, the hideaway seemed like paradise. They walked in the door and she saw it was pretty close with its greenery – plants and trees everywhere – incredibly lush. The tabletops were glass and the couches white leather.

Off to the right in the living room was a huge stone fireplace. Candles burned. Champagne sat chilled in a bucket on the table. Chocolate-dipped strawberries lay invitingly on a silver tray. Soft music played and roses stood in vases. The scene and mood was set.

Wayne took Heather's hand and guided her out the door onto a patio that overlooked the ocean. Outside a slight breeze caressed, her nipples soon hardening under her white silk blouse she had carefully chosen before being spirited away by Wayne.

Wayne seemed to notice and appreciate how the wind affected Heather.

He unbuttoned her blouse, allowing her bare skin and her naked breasts to feel fully the soft caress of the ocean breeze. He carefully cupped his hands over her breasts, then leaned toward her and took one of her stiff nipples in his mouth.

She enjoyed his wet lips as they tickled her skin and moistened her nipples. She could feel the wetness begin between her legs and the desire for him grow stronger. He pulled her white linen pants off her, leaving her only in her white thong panties and a hunger she desperately wanted to feed.

Wayne lay her down onto the lounge chair and kissed her body, sending shivers along her spine. He took her panties in his teeth and pulled them down her legs, driving her crazy with intense pleasure. He kissed her small patch of jet-black curls and then slowly dug his tongue in as far as it could go. He licked her, tenderly at first, but then increased the speed and pressure until her legs became jelly and she shuddered out of control.

Heather screamed so loud that Wayne startled briefly. But he continued licking her and sucking on her moist lips until she came in a burst of juices, which he thirstily drank up. As she lay enjoying her afterglow sensations, she watched Wayne take his clothes off and lay down next to her on the lounge chair. She reached over and gently touched his chest with her fingers, caressing his nipples, then kissing them. Her fingers trailed down his chest... to his firm stomach... to his patiently waiting and incredibly erect penis. She touched him gently, wrapping her hand around its firmness, moving her hand up and down, feeling his body move with pleasure. As she moved her hand up and down, she shifted position and brought her lips to the tip of his penis, placing it in her mouth, swirling her tongue around the edges, and when she felt him tense up, she swallowed him whole. She felt his body moving and twitching and listened to him moan in sublime enjoyment. She continued sucking on him, moving her lips up and down, licking him with her tongue and finally, as his body went into convulsion-like spasms, he came... and he came again, until white salty fluid dripped from her lips.

Wayne got up and handed her a white terry cloth robe that lay at the foot of the lounge chair. It felt soft against her skin. They held one another for a moment, staring into each other's eyes.

Finally Wayne spoke: "I love you, Heather. I've decided that it's not fair to my wife or to myself that I continue on this way. I've asked my wife for a divorce. I think she already knew this was coming. She didn't put up a fight, instead she thanked me for my honesty and then promised to take me for everything that I have, but it's really over."

Gazing out towards the water, Heather thought for a moment about what he had just told her and what this would mean for them, and she smiled.

"Wayne, I love you, too, and I've been waiting for this. I want to be with you, but I also want us to take our time. If you really do get a divorce and you truly want to be with me, then you will respect my wishes and accept that I don't want to rush into anything."

His silent hug was his assent.

They walked hand-in-hand down to the secluded beach. Along the water's edge Heather did a double take. She thought she saw a small table and two chairs set up for a romantic dinner. As they approached she saw a man dressed in waiter attire. As she neared the edge of the table the waiter pulled out the chair for Heather. She looked at Wayne with bemused and questioning eyes as she allowed herself to be seated.

He just smiled and said, "I did this for you. I hope you like it."

The waiter then served them and disappeared. They enjoyed a meal of salmon, wild rice, steamed vegetables and far too many glasses of wine. When the waiter reappeared, he set down a silver tray in front of Heather. On it laid a small turquoise box with a white bow, quite clearly from Tiffany's. Again, she looked up at Wayne. Again he smiled. "Open it, Heather."

She opened the box hesitantly only to find a tiny white card that read: "This is my promise to you. I love you and I want to marry you, but I want it whenever you feel you're ready. My promise to you is that the next time you open this box, it will have a ring that I hope you will want to wear forever. Love Wayne."

Dazed with happiness, Heather stood up from her chair, wavering slightly, then, as if in slow motion, she floated around the table towards Wayne, knelt down before him and kissed him. She lifted herself up and kissed his forehead, his cheek, and then gently placed her lips on his in a lingering kiss. He wrapped his arms around her and they kissed passionately until they fell onto the sand together. They tore at each other's clothing... desire consuming their every thought, and they made love on the beach as the ocean water threatened to cover them.

As he entered her, she held him tightly, her nails slightly scratching his back, not willing to let go for fear that the moment would end. They continued making love until they came together and the warmth of their juices overcame the chill of the water as it lapped up over their naked bodies.

They ran from the beach to the house, tightly holding hands, laughing playfully like two young children. Giggling and shivering, they cuddled next to the fire, and then grabbed the large blanket atop the wicker basket next to them. Wayne wrapped it around them both and after a while, Heather fell asleep in his arms.

The next morning they woke up, showered and shared a wonderful breakfast of French toast, strawberries and champagne. When they finished, they went for a leisurely walk along the beach, sharing their dreams, and talking about the future they hoped would be theirs.

Heather stopped suddenly and looked over at Wayne. "Thank you for this wonderful weekend," she said breathless. "I love you more now than ever and I can't wait for the day that we can truly be together."

He kissed her again and they walked hand-in-hand back to the house.

The Voyeur

From my apartment I watch her walk in the front door, drop her keys on the antique table, and throw her coat and briefcase on the couch.

Every evening is the same. She goes into the kitchen to check her messages, listens, then makes the same face that tells me she's clearly disappointed. After this, she pours herself a glass of wine, and then takes it with her to her bedroom to change. She places her glass carefully on the table next to her bed and turns to stare at herself in the full-length mirror on the wall. She looks at herself for a long time, twisting her hair around her finger, looking sad.

It's hard to tell what's going on inside her head.

Her routine continues. She unbuttons her blouse and walks over to the closet to hang it up. Following the blouse come the skirt, then, more slowly, her stockings.

But tonight is different. She stands in her panties and bra and starts rubbing her hand across her breasts.

I've never seen her do this before, it's incredibly sexy, I can feel myself start to warm up.

She unhooks her bra and takes if off, then she then slides out of her panties, dropping them to the floor. She's very tall with incredible legs that go on forever. Her thick black hair falls down her back in ringlets of curls. Her body is beautiful, but the way she acts sometimes I don't think she realizes it.

She goes back to the mirror and stares at herself, caressing her breasts, her stomach, and her neck, and then drops her hand slowly between her legs. Her head arches back as she starts rubbing her fingers back and forth. I am amazed by how much pleasure she is giving herself, the ecstasy on her face.

While she touches herself, I do the same. I close my eyes and pretend it's her hands all over my body. I look back into her apartment and I see that she's gone into the bathroom, and is pouring herself a steamy bubble bath.

She lights a few candles and turns out the lights. Carefully, she steps into the water and submerges herself in the bubbles. She tilts her head back against the wall. I can see her hand as it begins to caress her breasts again. I can't see where the other hand has gone, but I imagine that it's between her legs. I watch her close her eyes, and move around in the water... enjoying the pleasure she is giving herself.

This is driving me crazy; I'm in the dark of my apartment, completely naked. Touching my body, I imagine myself lying next to her, her skin slightly touching mine, our bodies moist with sweat, anxiously waiting to touch one another. I look up and see that she's out of the bathtub. Where is she? I can't see her anywhere; I check the bedroom, the kitchen, and the living room... oh, there she is... standing naked outside on the balcony. The brisk wind blows across her body. I wish I could touch her; I reach out towards her but I can't reach her. I watch as she walks back into the apartment; her breasts are so beautiful and her nipples are so hard. Her stomach is flat and the dip in her lower back reaches just slightly outwards to a perfectly round and well-toned bottom. She has such an incredible body.

She finishes her wine, pours another glass, and then walks over to the stereo. Her hand touches a button and she begins to dance. I can't hear the music but as I watch her swaying back and forth. I can almost feel it myself. She goes back into her bedroom and starts rummaging through a dresser drawer. What is she looking for? I can tell she's getting frustrated. She's throwing stuff all over the floor and is searching through the other drawers. She must have found whatever she was looking for. She holds it up and starts rubbing it against her stomach.

Oh, I see it now; she's brought out a toy for herself, and is clearly enjoying it. As she moves it up to her stomach, across to her breasts, and down between her legs, she climbs on top of the bed, lies on her back and places it inside her. She pushes it in and out and at the same time she pinches at her nipples and smiles, obviously enjoying herself.

I see the sweat glistening on her body in the light; her hair is wet and has started curling in little, messed-up ringlets around her head. Her stomach and chest are damp. She pulls her toy out and replaces it with her fingers holding them in one position for what seemed like forever. She takes her fingers out again and puts them into her mouth, slowly licking one finger at a time.

This woman is driving me nuts. I've never felt this kind of excitement before. I wish it were my mouth tasting her fingers. She lies there for a few minutes and slowly falls asleep. I watch her for quite some time, and then I fall asleep dreaming... wondering what she might taste like...I dream about her all evening; her body, her smile, her breasts.

The next day I met my boyfriend for breakfast and told him about the evening before. I admitted to my excitement while watching another female pleasure herself, that I longed for her to touch me. Suddenly aroused by our conversation, he grabbed my hand and placed it in his lap. I could feel how excited.

We went back to my place and made passionate love all afternoon long. That evening, when my neighbor came home, she followed the same routine and headed towards the answering machine. This time I saw her smile. It looked as if she was rewinding and replaying the message over and over again. She had finally received the message she was waiting for.

Later that evening, my boyfriend came over and together we watched as she prepared herself for the evening. This time she wasn't alone. A handsome man came over, bringing a beautiful bouquet of flowers and a bottle of red wine. She quickly took off his coat and threw it on the couch. She slowly unbuttoned his shirt, peeled it off his muscular shoulders, and tossed it on the floor. She unhooked his belt, unbuttoned the top button of his jeans and unzipped them. She pulled his pants off of him, leaving him there completely naked.

By his elated expression he was happy to see her, and we watched her show him how happy she was to see him. She quickly got up off her knees and turned off all the lights. We watched as she took off her clothes in front the large window that faces my apartment.

All of a sudden she seemed to be staring up at us, she grabbed a hold of her breasts and started fondling her nipple, gazing at us the whole time. She licked her lips, smiled at us, and then slowly reached up and closed the curtain. I was certain she knew I was watching her then, and that I had been watching her before.

My boyfriend and I made love that evening, more passionately then ever. I still couldn't help wondering what it would have been like to be laying next to her, our skin lightly touching. I think both of us women fulfilled a fantasy that evening. Hers was being watched and mine was watching, but when it came to making love to someone she cared about, she kept that to herself.

The Affair

After three years of seeing Mike, a married man, Heather decides to break it off. As if on cue, Mike sends flowers with an invitation for a weekend away at his house on the beach. At first Heather declines, but she is soon convinced otherwise.

He picks her up and they drive along the coast, holding hands, as Mike reassures her with promises of a romantic and sexual weekend.

When they get to the beach house, Mike brings out the already chilled champagne stocked in the fridge and they make love on the chaise lounge out on the deck that overlooks the ocean. They kiss and cuddle and take a walk on the beach. They have a wonderful dinner and settle before of the fire. They make love again, slowly and passionately. They fall asleep in each other's arms.

In the middle of the night the doorbell wakes her up. Mike is asleep and snoring, so Heather gets up and answers it. A tall, beautiful blond woman stands in the doorway, seemingly shocked to see Heather, as Heather is to see her. Apparently this is another one of Mike's girlfriends coming by the house to "surprise" him. The women talk for a while; comparing notes, then nod knowingly to each other with devious smiles.

When Mike wakes up, Heather and the other woman, Kelly, sit at the table, drinking coffee. He, too, is shocked to see them both at once. He tries to explain. It turns out Mike isn't married at all; it is just his excuse for not getting serious with anyone. After the women express their feelings, they say goodbye, grab a bottle of champagne and leave together in Kelly's bright red BMW.

Mike meanwhile has recapped the champagne and it is re-chilling in the fridge as he rifles through his little black book, then picks up the phone receiver. He dials. He smiles. He hangs up,

"Why waste a weekend and a beach house?" he muses aloud to himself.

a complimentary sample of:

NOW AVAILABLE IN SOFTBACK

from

deadendstreet.com

Afternoon Agenda

The dulcet chime of the mantle clock signaled the noon hour. Elsa, kneeling on the lush beige carpet in front of the entertainment center, immediately put aside her wool duster and stood up. As she rose her blonde hair fell in two long braids across the front of her shoulders to flank her naked pert breasts.

She longed to slip into the robe hanging behind the bathroom door, but Robert, her husband, only allowed her to wear it after showers or when certain visitors showed up. Otherwise, as now, she wore whatever he had selected for her the night before. Today it was soft pink thigh-high stockings and a matching silk collar with a dangling gold heart charm engraved with his name.

As custom, when he kissed her good-bye before leaving for work, he'd clamp a pair of little golden hoops to her nipples. The unrelenting pinch of the ornaments was a reminder to behave, for the only respite she had would come at bedtime (and then only if Robert decided she'd earned it). But Elsa was hardly concerned with the tug at her nipples, for the fragrance of patchouli and cinnamon still lingered in the house from incense she'd burned that morning, and its heady scents reminded her of the oil Robert patted on each morning.

Only a few hours had passed since he'd left, yet all she could think of was the virile smell of his skin and his roguish grin... and, of course, his smoldering chestnut eyes. There was a certain dangerous glint in Robert's eyes, and with a single glance he could make her feel completely naked.

Sighing, Elsa walked to the black leather bar that stood at one side of the living room. From the portable refrigerator hidden in the back she took an apple and a carton of vanilla yogurt. Although not very hungry, she knew the punishment for avoiding lunch would be severe, as Robert had already scolded her several times for the Spartan appetite her mother had instilled. He'd long since made her cast aside tofu and bean sprouts for meat and vegetables, promising she'd never be allowed to grow fat or flabby as long as he was alive. Besides, every glimpse in the mirror confirmed a shapely, still-girlish figure. Every morning she performed her exercises, especially the ones designed to keep her vaginal muscles taut.

Elsa hopped up on one of the bar stools and ate lunch. Just as she finished a knock sounded at the front door. Elsa deposited the apple core inside the empty carton and tiptoed to the bay window. Pulling aside the ivory linen curtain, she looked out to the front entryway and was shocked to see a familiar feminine profile and mop of red curls. *Diana...!*

Although Elsa hadn't seen her old friend in almost a year, she was reluctant to open the door. Robert had decided long before that Diana was never to set foot in their home even though Diana and Elsa had been raised practically as sisters. They had grown up within the isolated confines of the Sisterhood, an agricultural community founded by Elsa's mother and several of her ex-hippie, ultra-feminist companions. Having never embraced the group's ideologies, Elsa left the Sisterhood on her eighteenth birthday to seek out a more conventional life in town while Diana, opinionated and high-strung as a child, had developed into an exemplary member of the Sisterhood. She was a woman ever-ready to defend and promote the Sisterhood's fundamentals, and Elsa had no doubt that Diana would launch into a frothy tirade with but one look at how her childhood companion was dressed. Despite that, the woman was part of the only family Elsa had (besides Robert), and when she knocked again Elsa broke out in a cold sweat, wishing she'd simply forgotten Robert's instructions.

"Hey, Elsa! Don't tell me that Neanderthal has you tied to the stove!"

Elsa exhaled. She went to the door and opened it enough to peek out.

Diana beamed. "Well, stranger, didn't think you were going to let me in."

"Uh, hi... wait a moment and I'll throw something on..."

"Oh, don't be ridiculous! How many times have we seen each other in the buff?" And with that Diana pushed the door open and strolled in.

Elsa quickly closed the door. As Diana surveyed the living room furnishings, Elsa noticed Diana's taste in fashion had changed little since their youths. Although she had a voluptuous figure and pretty face, these attributes were purposely downplayed. She wore an oversized tie-dyed tee shirt and baggy denim shorts that reached to her knees. On her sunburnt feet was the same pair of crepe-soled flip-flops she'd worn for years, although the tattoo of the Willendorf goddess on the outside of her left ankle was a recent addition. Diana's fair skin was prematurely wrinkled from hours spent tilling fields, corralling goats and hogs, and chopping wood. Her red hair, which Elsa remembered as glossy and beautiful, was oily and windblown. Elsa was tempted to offer her a comb but decided not to risk it.

"Nice picture," Diana offered with a note of sarcasm, indicating the tapestry hanging above the sofa. It was a woven image of Apollo driving His chariot through the heavens while bearing a naked and frightened nymph over one shoulder. "I came to pick up supplies at the hardware store and thought I'd..." she turned to Elsa and her mouth fell open.

"My goddess... it's as bad as I imagined!"

Elsa walked past her into the living room and took a seat on the sofa. "I don't mind if you came by to chat," she sighed, gathering her knees to her chest and wrapping her arms about them. "But don't *even* try the amazon head trips. Having at last escaped the bonds of radical feminism, I have no desire to return to them."

Diana blinked as if too dismayed for words, although Elsa recognized the eagerness for debate in her blue eyes. "Bonds... why, look at you! *This* is how your husband makes you dress?"

"What's the real reason for the visit, Diana?"

Diana sat down at the end of the sofa. "I've been sent, as a representative, to ask why you've turned your back on us."

"The Sisterhood has none to blame but themselves. I invited you to my wedding, and the whole lot of you mocked my husband at the reception!"

Diana flipped an errant lock of hair over one shoulder. "The lot to whom you refer is your family... and we have only your best interests at heart. It is quite apparent that you need our guidance if you ever hope to re-empower yourself."

"I'm as empowered as I need or want to be. I have no desire to be part of a man-hating matriarchy... something you knew before coming here."

"That chauvinist has brainwashed you!"

"Don't bad-mouth my husband, Diana."

Diana gave a condescending smile. "You know, your mother has asked the council to consider having you deprogrammed."

The nape of Elsa's neck prickled hotly. "Kidnapping! That only proves how fanatical you all are!"

"Our's is a self-sustained community, proud of our emancipation from generations of male domination. But you've disregarded everything our mothers taught us, just to play house here in suburbia. You're nothing more than a kept woman, Elsa, and you have betrayed our entire sex."

Elsa rose from the sofa, shaking angrily. "I know about the Sisterhood's emancipation, how our mothers sought out men to beget a crew of little farmhands so they'd have time for such endeavors as protesting beauty pageants and calling in bomb threats to strip clubs. They're no advocates for women, just their brand of the gender. Now… if you have nothing more to offer than trite flak, I think its time to say good-bye."

Diana stood up and smiled slowly. "I think I'll endorse your mother's proposal."

"You were once my friend... you wouldn't dare!" Elsa's voice quavered now, for she knew all too well that her mother and her cronies were not above using heinous tactics to meet their ends.

Diana looked at her for several long moments. "I might reconsider," she said, her eyes canvassing Elsa's breasts, "if you give what you've always teased."

"And just what is that?" Elsa stammered, uncomfortable by the brazen insinuation.

Diana laughed and suddenly pushed her down on the sofa. Before Elsa could react Diana reached out and tore the golden hoops from her nipples. Elsa gasped, bringing her hands up to cover her throbbing breasts.

"The goddess provided men as resources to be utilized... only a woman knows how to truly gratify another. Its time you appeased Her will."

"Don't you dare whitewash your preferences with twisted dogma!" Elsa hissed.

Diana's callused hand struck her across the face. Tears rushed to Elsa's eyes, for she couldn't forget that once they had been as close as sisters. Diana kneeled between her legs and moved her hands up Elsa's thighs.

"Do those slinky little things make you feel more exposed than wearing nothing at all?" Diana asked, stroking the flesh beneath the stockings.

Elsa glanced around miserably, unable to reply.

Diana combed her fingers through the thatch at Elsa's pubis.

"Yes, I think it does... " Diana parted the dark blonde hair and separated the underlying folds of flesh beneath. Elsa's cheeks burned as Diana massaged the pink inner lips between her thumbs.

"Oh, Diana, don't!"

Diana replied by blowing on the fragile hood of Elsa's clitoris. With the stroke of a thumb Diana roused the tiny organ to attention. Elsa stirred fretfully, for the manipulation kindled a flame deep within that orifice which by rights belonged only to Robert. She panicked, thinking that somehow she was betraying him, and tried to wriggle away from the goading fingers. Diana immediately yanked her pubic hair, constraining her to be still.

"Good girl," Diana purred, relinquishing her hold. She spread Elsa's legs further apart, and leaning her head forward, grabbed Elsa's clit between her lips. With her tongue she kneaded demanding little circles about the organ. It swelled and pulsated beneath the pressure, and Elsa shivered, alarmed by the pleasure that coaxed her juices to flow against her will. Diana brought a hand to the moist lips and glided a forefinger through the quivering font. Elsa jolted against the intrusion, but Diana proceeded to work in another finger. She pumped the silken orifice vigorously as her lips continued to suckle the fluttering clit.

Elsa's eyes fell shut and her head sank back on the cushion. She found herself wanting to fondle her sore, hardened nipples. Her drenched sex almost lifted toward her tormentor as the relentless fingers plunged deeper and deeper. She cried out when Diana's knuckles pressed against her throbbing, needy core; and as Diana drove her toward the threshold Elsa felt her hips shamefully undulate and heard an urgent plead escape from her own lips.

But just as she readied for orgasm Diana drew her hand away.

Elsa's eyes flashed open. With a racing heart she watched as Diana pulled off her shirt. Her breasts were enormous creamy globes set with wide, tawny nipples. Diana stood to remove her shorts, then grabbed Elsa by one braid and forced her to kneel on the floor. She lifted Elsa's chin so that she was looking straight into the thicket of reddish curls between Diana's milky thighs. Elsa saw two succulent puckering lips peek through the curls and caught the musky scent of Diana's desire.

"Please me..." Diana crooned, delving a hand through the thicket.

Too frightened to object, Elsa drew open the wet lips. Diana's imposing clitoris jutted forth like a gleaming, offered berry. Elsa hesitated, again remembering her troth was to Robert. Yet, gaining her husband's forgiveness would prove easier than escaping the designs of the arrogant Sisterhood. She clasped Diana's hips and gingerly kissed the eager hot flesh. She tasted the salty lips and licked the pulsating clit. Diana sighed and released Elsa's hair, then bunching up her own breasts between her palms, suckled the large nipples. Elsa tested a finger through her damp cleft, then a second.

Diana gasped, and Elsa was reminded of something she'd seen once seen in a movie. She balled her right hand into a tight fist and pried it up into Diana's vagina. The woman's back arched and her muscles constricted about the hand as Elsa pumped at the orifice with deep, steady strokes.

"Ah, yes... faster!"

Elsa did as commanded, and Diana began to writhe in rhythm with the thrusts. Her fair skin was feverish now and dappled with perspiration. Knowing the woman was about to come, Elsa worked the cavity adamantly. Diana moaned, her nether muscles contracting tightly about Elsa like a vise. Elsa watched her clit shudder and felt Diana's juices spurt down her wrist as she rode out the orgasm. Elsa looked up and saw Diana's lips quiver, her cheeks as flush red as her hair. Diana's eyes were wide and unfocused. She seemed astonished.

Why, she looks as if this is her first orgasm!

But Elsa was not to reflect long; for moments later she heard someone at the front door.

Turning her head, her heart skipped a beat as Robert stepped into the house. His eyes fell on the two women and his briefcase dropped to the floor. Horrified, Elsa scooted away from Diana, who was already struggling for her shorts.

Robert approached them. He regarded Elsa sternly.

"What's going on here?"

Elsa's voice trembled in answer, "She said that if I didn't do what she wanted, I'd be kidnapped and deprogrammed by the Sisterhood!"

"Are you hurt?"

At her mute nod Robert gave a relieved sigh. His eyes turned to Diana and narrowed. "So you threatened her into reaming that cunt..."

"No," Diana smirked, "she *begged* for it."

Robert backed her into the wall. "I don't believe it, bull dyke."

Diana blanched with anger and lunged at his throat with clawed hands. Robert threw his hands up between her forearms, and, throwing them apart, slapped her open-handed across the face. Then, grabbing one of her wrists, he spun her around and shoved her down across the sofa, pinning her wrists to the small of her back. He pressed a forearm over her folded arms as she cursed and wrestled vainly for freedom. Peering down at her vulnerably exposed vagina he traced the still throbbing clitoris with the thumb of his free hand. Diana jolted, snarling. He snorted disgustedly, and slapped her soaked pussy lips.

Although Diana bristled at his touch, Elsa could tell by the slight sway of her hips and the agitated knit of her brow that the revulsion was mingled with desire.

"You new-age amazons will never concede that a man might have anything to offer a woman besides sperm," Robert said, slipping his hand down to unbutton and unzip his trousers. "Its time you were given a demonstration of those things the beast you loathe truly has to offer." Pushing down his trousers and his jockeys, he grasped the base his cock and rubbed the member between Diana's compressed thighs. Even as she cursed again, her hips strained toward him. Robert released one of her arms, and, as her struggle seemed forgotten, released the other. And as Diana awaited in perfect supplication, Robert looked to his wife as he began stroking his cock. Elsa saw that his desire was not for the woman kneeling before him, but her... and the stark lust in his dark eyes and the authoritarian set to his firm jaw sent a heated pang rippling through her thighs.

When Robert spoke to Diana again Elsa detected a baiting edge in his tone.

"Are you ready?"

Diana nodded, her hips rocking eagerly. "Yes."

Robert smiled at her response and seized her buttocks. Diana cast a troubled peek over one shoulder as he wrenched the fleshy cheeks apart and leveled the head of his cock at the dark rim of her anus.

"What are you doing?" she asked.

Without warning he plunged in. Diana lurched forward with a bestial cry. Robert secured her firmly by the hips and pounded at the unwilling orifice. She shrieked indignantly, her eyes bulging and mouth foaming.

"You bastard!"

Robert reached up and slapped the sides of her dangling breasts. "Be grateful I don't take your mouth instead!"

Elsa found she enjoyed the spectator's view of her husband's straining sinews and muscles as he worked his cock in and out of Diana's anus. As Diana whimpered under his savage thrusts Elsa's own sex hungered anew, and she reached with one hand to her still moist and titillated sex. But when Robert glanced over his disapproval was grave. She froze, bowing her head humbly, though her desire chafed like a firebrand in her nipples and between her legs.

Diana's demeanor had become one of resignation; only the faint pout of her lips betrayed her discomfort and humiliation. She was as pliant as a rag doll beneath Robert's hammering pelvis as he snatched the ends of her hair and forced her head back. He made a last, resolute lunge through her tight anus, and pulling out, grasped the shaft of his cock and yanked until his entire body tensed and his jism spurted over her back.

He rose to his feet seconds later and pulled up his jockeys and trousers. As he helped Elsa to her feet, Diana stood, shakily. She adjusted her clothing without uttering a word, but the encounter had left her cheeks scarlet, and Elsa suspected it would be some time before the color faded.

Robert addressed Diana icily. "When you get back to the farm, tell my mother-in-law that if she or any of her comrades even try to touch my wife, they'll receive a similar demonstration... only from some of my chauvinistic friends over at the sheriff's department."

Diana yanked the shirttail of the tie-dye over her shorts and ran a shaking hand through her hair. She remained silent as she made her way to the front door and turned the knob. But upon drawing the door open she shot Elsa a haughty glare.

"May the goddess curse you, traitor!"

Elsa shook her head. "Save it for the next council meeting, Diana."

Diana blinked, her mouth tightly pursed. Then she bolted out, slamming the door behind her. In a few moments Elsa heard another slam, that of a car door, followed by the revving of an engine and the squeal of tires across pavement. Robert went to the door, turned the lock and drew the bolt. He came back to Elsa and pulled her into an embrace.

"Are you alright?"

Elsa nodded, and she felt the distress of the confrontation wash away in the refuge of his strong, comforting arms. He kissed her brow, her cheeks, her lips. The taste of his mouth filled her with a familiar and weakening pleasure.

"You're too trusting, babe."

She nodded, feeling somewhat intoxicated by the virile smell of his skin. He squeezed her again, then taking her by the hand, led her toward the bar.

Elsa knew a moment's foreboding as he stood her before it, and her heart quickened as he lifted her hands and set them atop the vinyl counter. He bent her forward so that her back was straight and her braids hung down either side of her swaying breasts. She felt Robert's hand glide down the length of her spine and the breath caught in her chest.

"Now, I don't hold you responsible for what Diana did," he said mildly, and patted her buttocks. The heat of his palm made her wince. "But you disobeyed me by letting her in."

"Yes, sir."

"It must have been providence that made me take off early," he continued, slipping his hand down to her vulva. He massaged the swollen lips, and Elsa had to fight the urge to squirm her hips, knowing from experience that to show any reaction to such teasing would merit more punishment than he already planned. He leaned forward so that his face was close to her cheek.

"I doubt she would suddenly have been overwhelmed with a guilty conscience had I not walked through the door." He continued to work her sex, though he was careful not to touch the already impassioned clit. Elsa whimpered, shamed by the fluids streaming down her legs, regretful of her disobedience. Out of the corner of her eye she saw the smile on his face as if approving of the added frustration she was experiencing. But his breath was hot on the nape of her neck and she longed to turn and kiss him. She wanted him more than she had ever wanted him before, and as he slid a finger into her taut, wet nethermouth, her control faltered and her pelvis buckled slightly.

He had risen to his full height then, and withdrew his finger from her. He raised his arm and brought his outstretched hand down hard across her buttocks. She cried out; but of course, her cries held no sway over his will. He continued to punish her with brisk, hard spanks that nearly brought her feet off the floor. Her buttocks very soon felt as if they were blistering, for it had been a while since she had received such chastisement, and her hips danced frantically in the effort to dodge his aim. He responded by catching her about the waist with one arm, hindering her movements, and delivered a deluge of blows that resounded throughout the room. Elsa began to cry, as much for knowing she deserved such punishment as for the pain itself.

"Are you going to let that woman in our home again, young lady?" he asked, his hand never slacking in its task.

"No, sir!" Elsa sobbed. "I'm sorry, I'm sorry!"

"Whom *will* you let into the house?"

"Only those people you approve!"

Robert gave her another dozen or so resounding spanks before staying his hand. He stepped away, but Elsa did not budge from her position, even as she heard the disquieting sound of the curtain being drawn back from the bay window. When Robert returned, he lifted her by one arm and turned her toward him. Through her tears she saw that he held the nipple clamps in one hand.

"Were these removed by your own choice?"

Elsa shook her head earnestly.

"Good," he said and attached them back in place, giving each nipple a curt tug as he did so. Then he lifted her at the waist and laid her across the bar top so that her legs dangled above the floor and her breasts hovered over the other edge. He patted her tender buttocks and stepped to the side of the bar to where he could look at her tear stained face.

"I'm going to take a shower," he said. "When I get out you may cook dinner. But when dinner's over, expect to return to this position until bedtime. And if you've behaved until then, I might even consider giving that little pussy the attention it craves. Either way, your little butt *will* be kept sore and rosy all evening."

He turned and Elsa watched him walk down the hall to the bathroom. She sniffed back a last penitent tear, regretting the ceiling fan was not running and offering even a slight breeze to her throbbing bottom. The clamps were already serving their purpose of irritating her nipples as well as now making her breasts feel heavy and weighed down over the bar. The worst thing was knowing anyone passing by the bay window might glimpse her displayed over the bar. But she was determined to behave and not allow the discomfort or humiliating exposure make her irritable... because, despite everything that had happened, she ached for the fulfillment only her husband could provide.

a complimentary sample of:

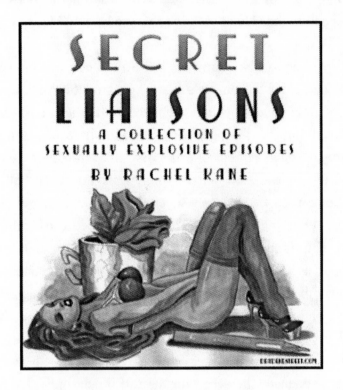

EBOOK NOW AVAILABLE

from

A Stranger in Paradise

As the evening sun began to cast a warm amber glow around her study, Alex leaned back from the computer and sighed. After writing all day, she knew that everything she'd written would eventually be rewritten.

She looked out of the window overlooking her and Danny's private beach, and watched the gentle lapping of the waves, the delicate white foam caressing the white sand, then retreating, leaving the sand dry within seconds. For such was the heat of that day.

Alex decided that she needed a dip in the water, the lower half of her body lying in the shallow warmth of the breaking waves, her upper body exposed to the still hot evening sun. She closed down the computer, picked up her cigarettes and glass of red wine, and went to find Danny. He was where she expected him – on the balcony that led from their bedroom – a pile of ledgers and papers spread out on the large wicker table at which he always did the accounts. She stopped as she entered the bedroom and stood quietly to watch him for a moment from the shadows, and deciding for the millionth time that he was the most beautiful man she had ever seen.

His naked torso was muscular and enveloped by taut golden tanned skin that shone with each rippling movement of his arm, however slight, as he studied the books, making notes now and again. He ran his hand through his black hair, the gesture creating the careless ruffle that made Alex want to mimic it with her own fingers to feel the soft thick strands caress the delicate skin on her inner fingers. She studied his body from top to toe, marveling again at his firm physique and his thick solid thighs that had so often rapturously trapped her own in their powerful grip during their lovemaking. His powerful arms were now behind his head, hands clasped and fingers linked. These arms could enclose her body so gently, yet hold her so firmly, and made her feel small and safe in his care.

He stretched and looked over and noticed her in the doorway. "Hi babe, have you finished writing?"

Alex advanced further into the room, taking a sip of the sweet wine, tasting the Spanish sun and clean air that had lovingly nurtured the grapes into this exquisite liquid. "Yep, well, for now anyway. I can't seem to get it right, it's so annoying, so many thoughts buzzing about. But they come out as crap the second I touch the keys."

He smiled lovingly and moved his chair back, holding out his arms familiarly for her to come and sit on his knee, one of her favorites among his repertoire of charming, easy gestures. She went to him, and wrapped her arms around his thick, tanned neck, while his arms encircled her waist.

"You're trying too hard, take a break for a while," he said. "Why don't you go and have a swim? That always relaxes you, and I can watch you floating from here, I love to watch you do that, you always look so... peaceful."

He kissed her lips briefly and tenderly. She returned the kiss, feeling the heat from his body penetrate her own. Though he had sat in the full heat of the sun for most of the afternoon, he, like she, had a tan resilient to burning. Danny and she had lived on this piece of paradise coast in a beautiful and uncommercial region of Ibiza for two years now, and, by now she knew how much he loved the heat throbbing against his skin. Alex felt its heat though, since she had been in her study most of the day, a study shaded by a overhanging roof from which cascaded exotic flowers that grew from long pots lining the edge. The sun still found it's way into every corner, but without the ferocity of the heat outside. All rooms of the villa were air-conditioned, but in her study, she only turned it on around midday until three or four in the afternoon when the sun moved slightly to the east, taking with it the glaring rays, and leaving soft shifting shades that cavorted against the glass objects in the room with kaleidoscopic effect.

"I was just about to take a swim. I thought I'd come and see if you want to join me?"

"I can't, well, not yet anyway. I have to get this done, I've been putting it off all week and I need to chase the publishers about this royalty check. It's even later than normal." Danny shuffled a group of invoices impatiently, before Alex pulled his arm back around her, smiling at him and placing a light kiss on his forehead.

"Well, I guess they think it's better earning interest in their bank account than in ours, babe. I'll leave you to look after my interests then, and go and have a swim! Come down when you've finished, and bring a few cold *San Miguel* with you, it's still damned hot."

She stood up, picked up her wine and stepped back into the cool bedroom, sipping the last drops of wine as she went. She quickly removed her thin cotton dress and pulled on her bathing suit, placed on the bed earlier by Maria, their housekeeper, who knew Alex took a swim every afternoon and would place a bathing suit or bikini on the bed. Alex smiled as she thought of Maria, the matronly woman who was the best housekeeper and cook on the island, and by now a firm friend as well. Maria also ensured that there was always a good supply of the 'Vino Tinto,' Alex's favorite Spanish wine. Its correct name was unpronounceable, and despite Maria's constant urging of pronunciation, the two women finally agreed to call it simply, 'Vino

Tinto.' Maria's brother, Miguel, had one of the best bars in Ibiza town, and always reserved a case of this gorgeous fluid for Alex at a much-reduced cost. In any other holiday destination, a glass of this wine would be expensive, even by the cheap cost of alcohol on the island, but for Alex, the cost never rose. In return for this, and many other favors freely and generously given, Alex and Danny often invited Maria, Miguel and their spouses and children over for un barbacoa en la playa. These beach barbecues were the highlight of many weekends. Alex and Danny loved the company of these people, who were funny, kind, considerate, and loving to their children, who in turn, loved to frolic in the sea or the pool that adjoined the conservatory.

Her thoughts were interrupted by Danny calling to her from the balcony, where his chair was still pulled back from the table, and she saw that he had been watching her undress.

"Why don't you leave that off and come back here?"

Alex laughed and pulled up the swimsuit to cover her breasts.

"Behave!" she called back. "You've got work to do, you aren't my agent for nothing you know! I expect a full day's work out of you, then later, I intend to sexually harass you."

"I'll take you to a tribunal, you demanding bitch!" Danny laughed as he pulled his chair back into its position against the table.

"Ah, but you're also my husband, so I will just say that I was demanding my nuptial rights."

"Point taken. Okay, I give in, harass me!" Danny playfully pulled down the front of his shorts and revealed his erect penis for a few seconds before pulling the shorts back up.

"You slut!" Alex called to him, "Just keep that warm for me, and don't go starting without me right? I'll be back soon, or you come down to the beach when you've finished. If you ask nicely, I might just let you make love to me in the sea."

"Oh, I'll ask nicely, promise." Danny smiled at her and picked up his pen.

"Okay, see you later, be good."

"I always am, aren't I?" he called.

Alex smiled. "Yeah, and your modesty's your best point babe."

Their stretch of private beach was a few seconds walk across the perfectly manicured lawns, then through the dunes. Soon she was on the sparkling white sand, and walking down to the shimmering blue-green water. As she walked into the warm ocean, she felt the tension of her frustrating writing session slip away. The further she walked into the water, the better she felt. The freedom of being alone, the warmth of the water, the heat of the sun, all combined to give her the inner peace that she only ever found here, in this place. As the water rose up to her waist, Alex felt the urge to feel it caress her skin directly. It was their own private beach, after all, and the feeling of the water on her naked body was exquisite. She peeled off her swimsuit and walked toward the shore, and threw it onto the sand before turning back. When she was waist deep again, she lay back, as if on a bed, and allowed her body to float on the surface of the water. She stretched out her arms and legs for maximum buoyancy, then closed her eyes and put her head just under the water's surface, so that all she could hear was the sound of the water lapping as the gentle waves rocked her prone body.

As she lay, lulled between sun and sea, she thought of Danny, and pictured his erect penis he had jokingly shown her from the balcony. Allowing her thoughts to drift further, she remembered the night before when they had made love on the beach, then in their pool. Danny was a fantastic lover – attentive, selfless, and incredible. He knew her body inside and out, and knew exactly where to touch, when, and how, to give her the long lingering pleasure that was always part of their lovemaking. When they first walked down to the beach last night, it was only for a swim and maybe to sit in the growing twilight for a while. But suddenly, as often happened, she looked at Danny, and needed him, right there, right then, so she had stood in the water until it was halfway up the calves of her legs, and she had asked him to lick her; to kneel in the surf and lick and suck her clitoris in the way that only he could do, that made her orgasm fast and intensely over his mouth.

She was wearing one of her short, clingy dresses, and he wordlessly knelt before her, lifted its hem with one hand, and with his other hand separated her labia to expose her stiffening clitoris. Then after licking it, lapping at it, he had taken it between his lips and sucked it into his mouth, his tongue working all the time around the sensitive edges, then upwards until the throbbing button was trapped in his mouth. He continued to suck, before inserting a finger into her wet opening. She groaned and bent her knees while spreading them to give him better access to her. His forefinger moved expertly inside her, caressing the walls of her vagina, rubbing gently, then harder, before slightly withdrawing until his fingertip was just inside, barely. Then with his thumb, he began to caress the area between her clitoris and her dripping entrance. When her orgasm came, he plunged both his forefinger and thumb into her and sucked her clitoris hard, feeling the muscles inside her contract before spurting hot cum fluid all over his fingers. Still panting, her heart racing from her orgasm, she knelt down facing Danny, and kissed him, her tongue finding his, and tasting her own juice still in his mouth.

She reached down into his shorts and released his huge erect cock, rubbing her hand over the tip before gently exploring the opening of the glans with one wet finger. He responded to her touch, groaning and closing his eyes. She told him to stand, and when he did, she took his now throbbing penis into her mouth, too aroused to start slowly with the teasing licks and sucks that she usually did. Instead she pushed her lips over the shaft until it was all the way into her mouth, his foreskin rubbing the back of her throat as he began to thrust in and out of her mouth. He put his hands into her hair and pulled her head gently as he pushed his cock deeper. Each time he pulled his hips backwards, she flicked her tongue around the shaft, keeping the pressure of her suck on him, until after what seemed like only minutes, he exploded his cum into her mouth, and she sucked it eagerly from him, tasting the salty fluid and drinking it down, still sucking and licking until his erection began to subside in her mouth. When she released him, he sat down in the water next to her, and kissed her, and just as she had tasted her orgasm in his mouth, he could now taste his own.

For a long time, the two sat like that, still clothed, next to each other allowing the sea to wash over them, not speaking, but not minding it. They enjoyed the companionable silence as they relaxed, satisfied, listening to the sounds of the ocean all around them.

After a few minutes, Danny stood up and said, "How about a drink? I could do with one after that! You're incredible babe." He smiled, and held out a hand to help her up.

"Thank you kind sir. We aim to please, and you're not so bad yourself, in fact, on a scale of one to ten, you're about sixty-two."

"I bet you say that to all the boys!" he said, as they laughed together, then slowly strolled out of the water and up to the house hand in hand.

Danny and Alex had been married for three years, after each took years to recover from their first failed marriages, Alex's amicably, Danny's not so. Because of his bitter divorce, Alex was pleasantly surprised that Danny had wanted to marry again. She herself had vowed never to marry again, but this was because she enjoyed the independence of being single. True, she didn't believe she would ever meet the fabled 'Mr. Right,' nor that such a person existed, except in the imagination of optimistic romantics. Until Danny had arrived in her life, her opinion of men was not too favorable, and she certainly didn't believe she would ever fall in love. Her first marriage had been for all the wrong reasons and had failed because these reasons couldn't sustain a permanent relationship. Thereafter, she didn't want such a relationship anyway.

She had various affairs, or perhaps better said, 'encounters,' for the men in her life since her divorce were basically sexual. Those experiences taught her far more about men than she ever knew. One of her discoveries was that while it was supposed women needed the most affection especially in matters of sex, it was not in her case. She had to lie to men she was sleeping with, had to assure them she loved them, had to nurse many a fragile ego, while secretly enjoying the role reversal. She knew it wasn't fair. She eventually stopped it after an ugly separation from a man who believed her to be in love with him. He was devastated, and this hurt her in turn. After that she ceased playing with her lovers' emotions, and was honest enough with her men never to promise what she couldn't give.

That all changed. When she met Danny, the unthinkable and impossible happened. She fell dangerously, totally in love with him, on the very first day she met him. For the first time in her life, she felt the tumultuous mixture of emotions that being in love with someone brings.

At first, she was scared he didn't love her back. Then, as their relationship developed, and her love deepened, she felt vulnerable, knowing how horrible the pain would be if he did, in fact, leave her. Many times she wondered how she would ever cope if he had an affair, times when she wondered why someone as wonderful as him wanted her. Yet throughout all, she was happier than she had ever imagined she could be. He loved her, she knew he did, and in time she needed his love as much as oxygen. Without him, she wouldn't be alive, merely existing. No man could ever replace him, a far cry from her previous belief that men were like buses, always another when the last one left. Her loyalty to him was as fierce as her love strong, and she knew she would never be unfaithful to him, or do anything to hurt him. The best thing was, she knew that all that was reciprocated, and for every strong, wonderful feeling he inspired in her, she inspired the same in him. A perfect thing, a perfect unity. And since Alex had become a successful author, they had lived here, in this paradise found.

Danny was her agent and business manager – also her motivator and ego prop when she suffered the terror of writers block. He inspired much of her work, sometimes without her realizing it. But she knew, as with most writers, sometimes a single sentence or action could trigger her imagination and a book would develop. He was a financial consultant before he had become her full time agent and manager, and as such had managed the revenue from her work. Exceptionally well. He had made some good investments for her, and these resulted in their moving to a villa built to their exacting specifications, satisfying their dream, the same dream they looked at in awe the night before as they returned home from the beach.

Before entering their villa, they paused to pull a few stray weeds from the abundant flowerbeds that bordered the lawns, then went to the terrace adjoining the pool. This adjoined the conservatory where there was a large 'fridge,' well stocked with drinks, and lots of ice.

"What do you want to drink?" Danny asked as Alex sat back on one of the lounger chairs.

"Anything, so long as it's cold and alcoholic," Alex replied as she sat on a lounge chair. She felt the warmth of the evening drying her dress as Danny handed her a tall glass of cerveza. She drank thirstily as she watched him sit on the lounger next to her. He, too, took a long drink, and sighed as the cold liquid cooled him.

"What do you want to do tonight?" Alex asked casually. They didn't often go out, but did often rent a movie or send out for take-away.

"Whatever, I don't mind. I'm quite happy to just sit here."

"Me, too, it's a nice evening isn't it? Listen to the cicadas..."

They listened for a few moments to the low pitch hum of the thousands of insects settling into their various habitats after a day of flitting around and basking in the heat.

"Fancy some music on?" Alex asked. Danny nodded, so she went into the house, to the living room where the CD player was, below shelf after shelf of CD's. It took her some time to find one that she wanted to listen to, but eventually she chose the *Delicate Sounds Of Thunder* CD, her favorite Pink Floyd. After flicking the switch that activated the speakers outside, she returned to the terrace.

When she got back to the terrace, she saw Danny standing on the other side of the pool speaking to a girl over the hedge. Their villa was isolated, and there were few passers-by, so they would often go over to the hedge to speak to someone on the road. But most were familiar to them, usually people from the nearby village, but Alex had never seen this girl before. She looked maybe eighteen or nineteen, and had the look typical of the Iberian women: the long dark hair, deep brown eyes and beautiful golden brown coloring. She was dressed in a vest top and shorts, and had some sort of rucksack, a large sort of rucksack, strapped to her back.

Danny turned and said, "Alex, this young lady seems to have got lost, she wants to know if there's any hostels nearby, but I don't think there are any, are there?"

Alex joined him at the hedge. "No, not that I know of. I think the nearest you might be likely to find one would be in Ibiza town."

The girl slipped the rucksack off her back and sighed, obviously tired, hot, disappointed, and seemingly lost. She had apparently gone in the wrong direction from the village. Not that there were many ways out of the village, which lay at the foot of the slight hill on which their villa stood. But the one the girl had taken led only here. It had been constructed when they had the villa built, and the villagers out for a walk, usually in the evening, used it as a route up into the hills that were accessible by dirt track where their road ended. Alex said that maybe the girl should have taken the road that was a few yards to the west side of the village, which led to the main roads where buses ran frequently into the town.

"Ha, no! Que hora es... sorry, I ask what time is it, por favor?" asked the girl.

Danny looked at his watch, "It's 8:30, and don't apologize, we speak a little Spanish although we aren't too good yet!"

The girl smiled, but still looked a little upset. "Gracias, Senor.

Tengo que irme..." she looked around her as though wondering where she should go from here.

"Sorry, I didn't understand that." said Danny.

"She said she had to go," Alex told Danny before she turned to the girl. "Do you speak much English?"

The girl nodded. "Si, Senora. I learn English, but maybe not too good!" she said smiling.

Alex smiled back, and said, "I think you speak English better than we speak Spanish! Would you like to stay and have a drink before you go? You look tired."

"Ah gracias Senora! I am, er, Thursday."

Danny laughed and said, "I think you mean thirsty."

"Si, thirsty." she repeated.

Danny walked over to where a gateway was set into the hedge and opened it for the girl, taking her backpack from her as she came through. The girl kept up a string of "Gracias, gracias" as Danny and Alex led the newcomer over to the terrace and offered her a seat. She sat down heavily, very weary.

"What would like to drink?" Danny asked her.

"A beer would be nice, gracias Senor."

"Please, call me Danny, and this is my wife Alex."

"I am Elena, mucho gusto."

"Igualamente." replied Alex. The girl stood and raised her hand to shake hands with each of them, then she sat down again beside Alex while Danny went to get beers for them all.

"Where are you from Elena?" Alex asked, draining the remnants of her drink.

"I am born in San Jose, is not too far, have you been there?"

"No, I haven't. I'm afraid I don't get much time to go anywhere.

I always seem to be working."

"Si, what is your work?"

"I'm an author."

The girl looked puzzled "I do not know 'author', que es eso?"

"It means, writer...escritor, autor."

"Ah si! Naturalmente... Is good? You like to be author?"

"I love it." Alex smiled and the girl gave a radiant smile in return.

Danny returned with beers, several in bottles in a large ice bucket. He prised the top off one and passed it to Elena, before sitting at the edge of the pool and placing his and Alex's opened bottles on the table.

"Gracias." said Elena, then she drank the entire bottle without pausing.

"Is that better?" asked Alex, laughing lightly at the girl's ability to down so much beer so quickly.

"Estupendo!" she said, after carefully stifling an imminent belch.

Danny quickly opened another and passed it to her, eliciting another few 'gracias'. She drank this more slowly, but visibly relaxed as she sank back into the padded chair.

"What are you doing here Elena?" Danny asked.

"I am a student, and I just wanted to, er, travel around a little. My, er, how you say 'novio'?" she looked questioningly at Alex, who replied, "Boyfriend."

"Si," she continued. "I am meeting my boyfriend soon, he is student also. We are going to Francia together for the holiday."

"Does he live around here?" Alex said, leaning further back into the chair, feeling cooler now the sun was disappearing over the hills.

"No, he is to come here from visiting his familia in the town. We were to meet at the hostel, but I must have gone on wrong road. Is no problem, I go soon and find bus."

"I really don't think there's going to be any buses by the time you've got back down to the village. They don't come too often."

The girl looked startled, as Alex made the instant decision to invite her to stay the night, then take her to the town by car in the morning. She suggested it to Elena, who initially looked doubtful.

"I would take you tonight, but our car is in the garage having repairs, and it won't be back until tomorrow." Alex added.

"I do not want to put you to any trouble..."

"No, no, it's no trouble, but if you'd rather not, we can call for a taxi maybe if we can find a number?" Alex wondered if maybe Elena didn't want to stay, but equally didn't want to offend her by refusing her offer. After all, Alex thought, for all she knows, we could be mad axe murderers or something.

"Oh no, it is kind of you, but are you sure is no trouble to you?" Elena looked questioningly from Alex to Danny, and both shook there heads and reassured her that it was no trouble at all.

"Estoy muy agradecido."

"You're welcome. Now, would you like anything to eat?" Alex asked.

"No, no, really. I had some er, pasta, in the town, but thank you."

Alex settled back into her chair, and for the remainder of the daylight, the three chatted about where they were from, their families, and the usual small talk customary between hosts and unexpected guests. By 10:30 PM, the light had almost gone, and the automatic dusk lights came on around the pool. Elena jumped a little when they first came on, then giggled. Alex too giggled at her gesture, and supposed it was the booze making her giggly, its usual effect on her.

"Oh, they are pretty lights!" said Elena, still giggling nervously.

By now, all three had consumed fairly large amounts of San Miguel, and had then moved onto a bottle of the famed Vino Tinto, which Elena agreed was the best red wine she had ever tasted. Danny though hadn't drunk as much as they. He rose from poolside and said that he was going to go and finish up some work from earlier, and said that he would then go to bed.

Alex kissed him as he leaned over her. "Okay, but don't work too hard. I'll be up soon."

"Buenos noches Danny." said Elena, and he repeated the phrase in return.

"He is nice man, your Danny."

"I think so." laughed Alex.

"If you wish to go to sleep, that is fine with me, I..."

"No, no," Alex interrupted her, "I'm not tired yet. Do you want me to show you to your room now or later?"

"Later will be good. It is nice, sitting here, it's cool."

Alex nodded and reached over to pour Elena another glass of wine, which drained the bottle. As she rose to get another from the conservatory, she stumbled slightly, and Elena jumped up and grabbed at the empty bottle so that it didn't fall to the floor.

"Thanks, I would have dropped it!"

"Is no problem... I will come with you to make sure you do not drop full one, si? Is too good to be spilled!"

"Si!" Alex replied, and the two women walked together into the conservatory, giggling again.

When they got inside, Elena looked around and told Alex how beautiful the room was, touching the ornamental statues and glass figurines that lay around the window sills as she spoke.

"Thanks, I chose most of them myself, but some were gifts from family," she replied as she went over to the fridge where in a rack next to it, lay the wine. Before she took out a bottle, she asked Elena if she would prefer white wine, or rose perhaps. Elena walked over to where Alex was bending over the wine rack, and looked at the various bottles, pulling one after the other slightly out to read the label.

"You will have to decide, is too many to choose!" Alex laughed and pulled out another bottle of her special Vino Tinto.

"Well, if it's up to me, it's another of these."

Elena smiled and said, "Is a good choice! Shall I carry it, or are you more straighter now?"

Elena's incorrect speech and the double entendre made Alex laugh even more, so much so she had to sit down on one of the wicker basket chairs for a few moments to recover herself.

Elena placed the bottle on the window sill, and knelt in front of Alex. "Que pasa?" she said, laughing at Alex laughing.

"Oh nothing, it's just me being silly... it's just in English, straight means two things, it means upright, like you meant, but it also means not being gay."

"Gay? Is that happy?" said Elena, looking confused, but still giggling.

"No, well, yes, but it also means homosexual"

Elena's faced recognized the humor of her words, and said, "Si, si, is meaning are you more homosexual!" She busted up in uproarious laughter leaning her back against the chair that Alex was sitting on, until the laughing subsided, and Alex rose, picking up the bottle as she went, with Elena following her onto the terrace.

"Can I ask something?" said Elena as she took the proffered

glass of wine.

"Sure, what is it?"

"Would be okay if I swim in your pool? It has been hot today and..."

"Yes, of course, help yourself! Would you like me to get you a swimsuit?"

"No, I can swim... desnudo, what is the word.... naked, yes?"

"Yes, sure." said Alex, but her words were redundant as Elena was already taking the vest top over her head, revealing full large breasts, and large brown nipples. Then, as Alex sat down, Elena undid the button and zip on her shorts, while simultaneously sliding off her sandals, and left them where they fell.

"Why not you come and swim?"

Alex looked up from her glass, and considered for a moment before standing up. "I think I will, what the hell!"

It wasn't that nudity was unusual here, for many people bathed naked in the sea at various parts of the island, indeed she did herself, but not in public, only on their own stretch of beach. In that instant though, she decided that what little prudishness she had could go hang. It had been hot, and a swim naked would be very nice. As she removed her dress, she was conscious of two things – firstly that both she and Elena hadn't been wearing any underwear, and secondly, that Elena was watching her. What startled her, was Alex liked this attention. She liked the thought of this young, attractive girl looking at her body.

"God, get a grip!" she thought, and walked over to the steps down to the pool, followed by Elena. This was something else that happened when she drank too much, she felt randy, although it was usual for Danny to be there to cater to that whim. This was the first time that she had felt the stirrings of arousal in the company of another woman, but she tried to ignore it as they both entered the water, and she tried even harder not to look at Elena's body.

The two swam a couple of lengths of the pool, and then swam to the side where it was shallow enough to stand, and leaned back against the rail.

"Shall I bring the wine?" Elena asked, and Alex nodded, then watched as Elena walked up the steps, then over to the table where she picked up the bottle and the glasses and turned around and back down the steps. As she did so, Alex noticed that Elena had shaved off her pubic hair, and the protruding lips of her vagina were clearly visible as she entered the shallow water, then disappeared as she waded through the waist deep water to the rail. Elena placed the bottle and glasses on the tiled surround of the pools edge, and poured out a glass each, passing Alex hers, then clinking her glass against Alex's she said, "Hasta ahora!" and Alex repeated the toast, "To this day!" and took a large gulp of the wine.

For a few moments, the two women drank and remained silent, Elena running her hand through the water occasionally.

Elena broke the silence. "May I ask you, what is your age?"

"Er, yes, I'm thirty." Alex replied.

"Thirty? You do not look this age! It must be the good sun and the good wine!" she laughed.

"Thank you, it's very kind of you to say so, but I think I do look thirty. In fact, some days I look about ninety!"

"Pah! You are a beautiful woman, you should not say such things!" Elena playfully nudged Alex's arm, then casually, as though accidentally, Elena's fingertips brushed the top of Alex's breast, perhaps unintentionally, perhaps not. But Elena's fingers lingered longer than necessary, and Alex knew that if she had moved or made any remark, Elena would have immediately withdrawn her hand and the incident would have been passed off as accidental.

Alex didn't move. Instead, she looked at the long fingers, with their perfectly shaped white nails, moving incredibly slowly.

She watched mesmerized, her breath held, as those elegant fingers moved down, until they had traced their way over the rise of her upper breast, and were moving exquisitely slowly towards her nipple, which was now fully erect because of the gentle shivering caused by Elena's light touch. Only when Elena held Alex's nipple between her fingers and caressed it gently, did Alex release a shuddering breath.

"Is this nice?" Elena whispered, her mouth brushing against the lobe of Alex's ear.

Alex could only nod, then she closed her eyes and leaned her head back so that it rested on the tiles at the edge. Elena moved closer, her mouth now kissing and licking Alex's neck, and her hand now cupping Alex's right breast, holding it, as though feeling the weight against the palm of her hand.

"Your breasts are beautiful." she breathed, as she moved in the water until her body was pressed against Alex's, their breasts rubbing together. Elena reached up and pulled Alex's face towards her own, then began to kiss her lips, gently at first, just kissing the outside of her lips, then more forcefully pushing her sweet tasting tongue into Alex's mouth and finding no resistance to the rising passion in Elena's kiss. As they kissed, Elena reached down and caressed both Alex's breasts; and then breaking away from the kiss, Elena leaned over and took one of Alex's nipples into her mouth, sucking it. The ecstasy that Alex felt coursed through her body – the softness of a woman's lips on her breasts was an incredibly erotic feeling, and she simply closed her eyes, relishing every movement of Elena's tongue and lips, needing her to suck harder, but unable to move or speak. Elena continued to lick and suck Alex's breasts, her mouth moving over every part, as her left hand moved slowly down into the water, then began soft circular movements against Alex's stomach, as she moved relentlessly downwards. Alex arched her back, lifting her hips to enable Elena's hand to reach her pussy faster, but Elena was going to make this slow.

For what seemed a lifetime, Elena's hand lingered over Alex's stomach and hips, then down to her thighs, across her buttocks, squeezing the wet flesh, until finally, she put her hand in between Alex's thighs and pushed them gently apart. Alex needed no persuasion and parted her legs eagerly, desperate now to feel Elena's fingers on her vagina. Her clitoris throbbed, and she could feel an ache deep inside her that she knew meant that she needed penetrating; she needed to be touched inside. Elena spoke softly to her, asking if this was what she wanted.

"Yes, oh yes, please, put your fingers inside me..."

Alex reached down and took hold of Elena's hand, forcing it against the hot wetness of her opening, then rubbing herself on the palm of Elena's hand. Elena squeezed the labia, filling the palm of her hand with Alex's pussy, then with her thumb, she pushed back the lips surrounding Alex's clitoris, and made circular rubbing movements on the tip of the throbbing button..." Oh God, fuck me Elena, please..." then Elena suddenly, and with none of her previous gentleness, forced two of her fingers into the tight opening of Alex's vagina, causing her to draw a sharp breath as she felt Elena's nails digging into the delicate skin inside her vagina, but still thrusting out her hips, wanting the penetrating fingers to go deeper.

"Is this what you want Alex? You want me to fuck you hard, yes?"

Elena now pushed her hips against Alex's pubic mound, their clitorises grinding together from the forcefulness of Elena's movements.

"Yes, oh yes... I want to come, oh God, I'm going to come... aahh!" As her orgasm rushed out of her, Elena leaned against Alex's body hard and whispered into her ear, "You sexy bitch, your cum is all over me... you like to be fucked by a woman, yes? You want it again don't you?"

Alex could barely breath as this wonderful woman's exotic, sensual smell filled the air, and she could only nod in answer to Elena's questions.

"Turn around and lie on the edge... yes, that's it, lie on the tiles so I can see you...nice."

Alex did as she was commanded, and submitted willingly when Elena forced her legs apart, spread-eagling her over the tiles of the pool's edge. Elena was still standing in the pool, but Alex could feel the closeness of her mouth as it almost touched her pussy.

"Oh, bello... you are beautiful, open wider so I can see...oh, yes..." Elena's fingers spread Alex's labia so wide that it was almost, but not quite, painful. Alex felt pure sexual energy spreading through her again as she knew that Elena was looking at, and enjoying the sight of, her vagina, wantonly exposed, nothing hidden.

"I want to taste this, will you let me lick you?"

"Yes, oh God...."

Elena's tongue licked the sensitive inner lips around her soaking opening.

"Ooh, you taste so nice... mmm, lift your hips up, yes that's it"

Elena buried her face into Alex's vagina and rubbed her open mouth against her wetness, licking her hard, as a child licks an iced lollipop, before putting the tip of her tongue teasingly against the wide open pussy, licking and pushing just the tip inside, wriggling it until Alex could stand the agony of being teased no longer and began to push her hips backwards, forcing herself onto Elena's tongue.

When she felt the soft probing tongue enter her, she arched her back and instantly orgasmed, totally involuntarily, because she had wanted that exquisite building of her climax to last longer, much longer.

"You cum again, yes? You are a horny bitch. Turn on your back."

Again, Alex wordlessly obeyed, and opened her eyes to watch as Elena climbed out of the pool and sat astride her body. Elena was positioned so that her naked pussy was pressing against Alex's stomach, and she could feel that Elena was incredibly wet, and it wasn't the wetness from being in the pool, it was her juice, and as Elena moved up Alex's body, she could feel a trail of sticky fluid rapidly drying on her skin. As Elena moved further, she paused against Alex's breasts, rubbing herself on them, one at a time, groaning as the nipples rubbed her clitoris, then she straddled Alex's face.

"Lick me." The words were said huskily, and Alex instantly obeyed, opening her mouth while Elena lowered her body so that she could be licked. Elena reached down between her legs and spread her own labia wide open.

"See me? Is nice, si? Lick it... mmm, oh bella, yes, now suck it... oh that is so good..."

Alex could taste Elena's spicy juice all over her lips as she sucked on her large, swollen clitoris until she felt it begin to throb in her lips. She pressed her tongue hard against the mound and licked it, pushing it upwards, forcing Elena to move her hips to and fro with the movements of her mouth. Alex had never had oral sex with a woman before, but knew that this was one of the most erotic, incredible things she had ever done. Elena's vaginal juice was hot and smelled so sexy as it filled her mouth and covered her face. Elena leaned back, opening her legs wider, exposing more of her gorgeous pussy to be licked, and as she leaned backwards, her hand rubbed and caressed Alex's pussy again, her fingers finding the entrance and fingering it.

"Oh si, si, don't stop, lick it harder... put your tongue in me... your pussy is so wet, oohhh..."

Elena's shaven pussy was easy to lick, and Alex did so. Her tongue probed all of Elena's pussy, over and over again, until finally, she pushed her tongue in as far as it would go, then Elena orgasmed, her fluid just spurting out of her, gushing down her thighs and over Alex's face. As she came, Elena pushed her fingers deeply inside Alex, and she too orgasmed again, feeling the racing of her heart as her body expelled copious amounts of fluid onto this beautiful, exciting, young woman's hand.

After a few moments, Elena slowly withdrew her fingers and moved until she was sitting next to Alex who was still lying on her back, her eyes closed. Neither spoke for what seemed an eternity, and the only sounds in the settling darkness were the contented buzzing of the cicadas, the sounds of the ocean, the fluttering of palms in the gentle breeze and the slowing into natural rhythm of the breath of these two women, who had just lost themselves and their surroundings in the mutual joy of discovering each others bodies.

It was Elena who broke the silence. "Was that good? Was your first time yes?"

"With a woman?" As soon as she had said it, Alex realized that was a stupid thing to say, what else would Elena have meant?

"Si."

"Yes, it was the first time, and yes, it was good... incredibly good." Elena smiled broadly and knelt down and kissed Alex lightly on the lips.

"I am happy that you like this. Is good to do new things yes?"

Alex laughed at the way that statement had sounded – so matter of fact, so casual, like one might enquire how a recommended recipe had turned out.

"Yeah, it is, in fact, if new things are that good, I might try building a garage next week, I've never done that before either."

Elena too began to laugh now as she slipped back into the water, pulling Alex's ankles until she began to slide into the water.

"You make the fun of me!"

Elena began to splash the water towards Alex, who splashed back, the two allowing themselves to enjoy this childish pastime to the full.

They were unaware that they were being watched. In fact, throughout this entire time, ever since Elena and Alex first slid into the pool together, they had been watched.

After Danny had left the pool, he had gone to the balcony and resumed looking checking through the latest bank statements. After sometime spent checking stubs in the checkbook with their corresponding entries on the statement, he had noticed a blank stub, a £250 check. Danny had gone back into the bedroom intending to call down to Alex and ask if she could remember to whom it had been payable. When he got there, he opened the windows that overlooked the pool and terrace, and had been about to call down to Alex when he had seen Elena caressing his wife's naked breasts.

For an interminable time, though less than an hour, he stood at the window, aware he was unseen, so engrossed were his wife and Elena in their enjoyment of each other. At first, the sight was so unexpected, it rooted him to the spot as he stared at the scene unfolding below him. In moments that initial shock turned to arousal. As he watched his wife and Elena making love, first in the water, then on the side of the pool, he had gone from stirrings of arousal, to a throbbing erection that needed to be squeezed and rubbed, to final and explosive orgasm over his stomach as his wife had oral sex with this beautiful teenager. He continued to watch as they slid playfully into the water again, and splashed water at each other, totally unselfconscious of their nakedness or the erotic movement of their breasts against the water, then against each other again, their bodies again entwined, as they kissed passionately.

Alex and Elena had made love again then, this time on the loungers, and still Danny watched. He watched the two having sex together in different positions and places all around the terrace, until it was after midnight, when the two women had walked – or rather, staggered, for they were obviously drunk – into the house together, still naked, but holding their clothes casually in one hand as they chatted and sipped wine before disappearing into the conservatory. As Danny stepped back from the window and towards the en suite shower room, he could still make out the sounds of their voices, punctuated by bursts of laughter and intermingled with the dull beat of the CD player, until 2am, when the women lurched up the stairs, exaggeratedly shushing each other, then the sound of Elena whispering, then the door to the guest room closing.

By that time, Danny had showered and had lain on the bed, replaying in his mind the sight of his Alex and the exotic stranger Elena, making love, until he had to force himself to think of something else, aware that continuing to remember it would undoubtedly make him cum again, and he wanted to ensure that he was ready to make love to Alex the second she came up to bed. As the time moved inexorably slowly, when Alex finally opened the door to their room and crept in, his first impulse was to pull her onto the bed and make love to her, there and then with no prelude, just lay her down and enter her body. Instead, he feigned sleep, a split second decision, recalling a similar night in the past when he had done the same when she had stumbled into bed drunk on Vino Tinto. As he expected, she was asleep within minutes of stumbling into the room, her naked body stretched out on top of the bed.

Alex had always got turned on the next day when he had told her about screwing her while she was asleep... she always said how erotic it was to know that he had just taken her; used her body to satisfy himself.

She was lying on her stomach, and as soon as Danny heard her breathing settle into the pattern of one who is soundly asleep, he knelt in between her long tanned legs, separating them gently with his own, then silently but urgently, he penetrated her, pushing his cock into her, slowly thrusting, waiting to see if she would wake. She didn't. She was so fast asleep that even when his thrusting became harder and faster, his movements shaking the bed, still she didn't move or register any sign of wakefulness. All to quickly, whilst visualizing the sights of the earlier meage, and seeking out Alex's breasts to squeeze and caress, Danny spurted his hot fluid deep inside his wife, his ejaculation almost painful in it's intensity.

Danny rolled over and lay on his back, perspiration covering his body in a cooling sheen, until a few minutes later, he placed his arm around Alex's waist, and fell deeply asleep at her side, as they did every night. His last waking thought was that he hoped Elena didn't have to go too soon.

THE WANTING

take me.
take me now.
take me back into that wonder…
where you kissed me into orgasmic splendor,
into that point where i was no more separate.

take me.
grasp me with both hands…
pulling deep into passion never known before,
filling my body with yours til i rained down over you
in such sweet joy
mere words cannot describe.

take me.
and let me take you.
awash in a sea of heady waves
one after another after another...
after another.
so divine.

losing all 'semblance of room, walls, earth or sky.
as reason shatters
and logic is lost beyond this very moment.
losing myself in you
and knowing
i had found perfection.

ANOTHER FINE OFFERING FROM

DEAD END STREET, LLC.

Printed in the United States
127827LV00005B/15/A